WARRIORS
OF VIRTUE ™

Yun and the Sea Serpent

WARRIORS
OF VIRTUE ™

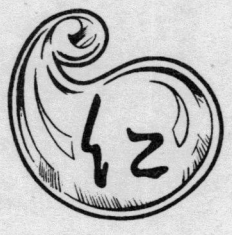

Yun and the Sea Serpent

John Vornholt

BOULEVARD BOOKS, NEW YORK

WARRIORS OF VIRTUE: YUN AND THE SEA SERPENT

A Boulevard Book / published by arrangement with
IJL Creations, Inc. and Law Brothers Entertainment International, Ltd.

PRINTING HISTORY
Boulevard edition / June 1997

The Putnam Berkley World Wide Web site address is
http://www.berkley.com

ISBN: 1-57297-283-1

BOULEVARD
Boulevard Books are published by The Berkley Publishing Group,
200 Madison Avenue, New York, New York 10016.
BOULEVARD and its logo are trademarks
belonging to Berkley Publishing Corporation.

PRINTED IN THE UNITED STATES OF AMERICA

10 9 8 7 6 5 4 3 2 1

chapter 1

RYAN HURRIED ACROSS THE PRACTICE field, running as quickly as his bad leg and heavy backpack would let him. The dark-haired thirteen-year-old wasn't a graceful runner, but he liked to go fast, ever since his visit to Tao. Before, he hadn't wanted people to see him run, but now he didn't care. So he had a limp—*they* could deal with it.

He glanced down the hill at Albright Middle School and the stadium, which was gloriously empty on this fine autumn day. Golden-red leaves sailed through the air like a fleet of kites, and he could smell spruce logs burning in a fireplace. What a wonderful day *not* to have football practice!

The coach had promised the team a day off if they won the big game against Central, and they had won it! So there was no practice. It was a miracle.

As one of the assistants, Ryan often had to stay later than the players. He always had a million tasks to do, from equipment repair to editing game tapes. But today he could finally spend an afternoon with Tracy, and tell her more about Tao.

Not that he was sure she believed him. But she hadn't run away screaming yet.

He saw her in the distance, at the top of the hill, where the gate opened into a small woods behind the school grounds. Tracy, wearing a plaid skirt and a red sweater and scarf, was looking very seasonal too. With a cheery smile, she turned to wave at him, and Ryan ran all the harder.

He was almost there when a voice behind him yelled, "Hey, Ry! Wait up!"

Ryan stopped cold and turned to see Chucky chugging up the hill after him. The chubby teenager was probably the only guy in town Ryan could outrun. But he wouldn't, because Chucky was his best friend.

Still Ryan scowled when he got closer. "What are you doing?" he whispered. "I didn't invite *you* along."

"But you're going to talk about that Tao place, right?" asked Chucky with a grin. "I love those stories!"

"They're not stories," insisted Ryan. "And me and Tracy—we wanted to be—"

"Hi, Chucky!" called Tracy as she skipped down the hill toward them. Now it was too late, thought

Ryan. If he chased Chucky away, it would be awkward.

"Hiya, Trace!" he called back.

"Hello, Ryan." She stopped and gave him a shy smile. "Are you enjoying your day off from practice?"

"I *was*," he answered with a pointed glance at his friend.

But Chucky didn't notice, as he dropped into a crunchy bed of leaves resting against the fence. "He's going to tell us those cool stories about the kung fu kangaroos!"

Ryan winced and looked helplessly at Tracy, who gave him an encouraging smile. They enjoyed hearing about his adventures in Tao, but they thought he was making it all up. Ryan had to admit, the stories did seem a little far-fetched, but he really had been there! They would never understand.

"They weren't kangaroos," he said. "Well, maybe they're related to kangaroos—let's call them Rooz. But it's even more than that; the whole land of Tao is amazing. They don't have cities—they have villages built around *Lifesprings*."

"Lifesprings?" asked Tracy.

Ryan grinned at the memory. "Think of a fountain that's full of light—in a pond that's bubbling with light. There are all these terraces and winding streams where this glowing water flows. Huge trees grow like crazy, and people live in tree houses, like a village."

"Are all the Lifesprings like that?" asked Tracy in wonder.

Ryan shrugged. "They were dead when I got there, except for one. This bad guy named Komodo was stealing the Zubrium from the Lifesprings in order to live forever."

"Zubrium?" asked Tracy.

"A mineral gathered by tiny creatures who live in the water. Master Chung said it was like coral in our world. Zubrium is the most precious substance on Tao—the Lifesprings need it to grow and be healthy."

He went on, "It all started when Ming, my friend from the Chinese restaurant, gave me a book. This book is called the Manuscript, and it took me to Tao. I got there in the middle of a war, when Komodo was attacking the last Lifespring, in the Radius of Green.

"On one side was Komodo and all his generals, soldiers and spies. On the other side was Master Chung and the Warriors of Virtue. Because all of us worked together, we were able to defeat Komodo."

"Yeah!" said Chunky. "I love that story—but not the part where Master Chung dies. Why don't you change it this time and let him live?"

Ryan shook his head at the futility of making them believe him. "It isn't a story—I can't change it. I wish I could take you there, but I can't."

"You do a very good job of taking us there," said

Yun and the Sea Serpent

Tracy, leaning against the fence. She was being nice, but Ryan still felt as if he was telling bedtime stories to his nieces and nephews.

"What was that one Roo's name?" asked Chucky. "The one who had the hoops?"

Ryan rolled his eyes. "Yee."

"Right! He was the boss, huh?"

"No, that was *Yun*," answered Ryan, trying to be patient. "Yun wasn't really the boss; he was just their natural leader. Let me start at the beginning, when I first got there—"

"Which one wears the medallion?"

Ryan groaned. "They *all* wear medallions. Please, Chucky, let me tell the story—"

Before he could say another word, Ryan heard footsteps crunching through leaves in the forest. He looked up to see two hulking figures striding toward them through the trees. Oh no! Could things get any worse?

It was Brad and Toby, two of the football players. They had a day off from practice too. Toby was a big fullback with a buzz haircut, and he was usually fun to be around. Brad was the star of the team, the quarterback, and he never let anyone forget it.

"See, I told you they were here," Toby said to Brad. He waved to Ryan. "Hey, big guy, are you telling those radical stories again?"

5

Ryan sighed. "That was the plan, but I didn't expect so many people to show up."

"Maybe you should sell tickets." Brad stepped through the gate and gazed at Tracy. He pushed his wavy blond hair off his tanned forehead. "Hi, Tracy, good to see you. That color is very pretty on you."

Ryan winced. Why hadn't *he* said that? He thought of it first.

"Thanks," answered Tracy, barely giving Brad a glance. She smiled at Ryan. "We do keep interrupting you. Sorry."

"Hey, let's not interrupt the storyteller, whatever we do." Brad crossed his arms and waited.

"Wait until you hear about the Kung Fu kangaroos!" crowed Toby.

"They weren't kangaroos," said Ryan, beginning to get angry. "They're called Warmbloods, and they're related to animals in our world—kangaroos, yaks, lions. But they're different, more like people."

"Hey, I know this story!" said Brad. "They keep the real people locked up in cages, and use them as slaves, right?"

"No!" growled Ryan. "It's not like that at all. The Warmbloods and the people live together in the same Lifesprings. The people are their friends and neighbors, although there are bad people too."

Brad scowled. "What do you mean? These animal

dudes are the *good guys,* and the people are the *bad guys*? This is a stupid story."

"It's not a story!" insisted Ryan. Without knowing what he was doing, he jumped toward Brad and stopped just under his chin. It was tempting to think about hitting that face, but Ryan couldn't do it. The Warriors had taught him to try other methods first, before resorting to violence.

Surprised, Brad took a step back. Then he narrowed his eyes at Ryan. "Watch yourself, water boy."

Tracy glared at Brad. "Why don't you let Ryan tell the story? That's why we all came here, isn't it?"

"Yeah," said Chucky with a nervous laugh. "He tells it real good, you'll see."

"Does this story have a title?" asked Brad. "Like 'I Was Abducted by Alien Kangaroos!'" He laughed at his own stupid joke, and Toby joined in.

Ryan wanted to smash Brad's face, but he saw that the bully's hands were balled into fists. An attack was just what Brad wanted, so he could beat Ryan to a pulp in front of Tracy.

"Okay," said Ryan, backing off. "You know it better than I do—*you* tell the story."

If you offered Brad the chance to be center stage, he never turned it down. He paced in front of the fence, acting important. "As I remember it, these animal dudes were mostly gorillas and lizard men, with big

7

fangs. There weren't any kangaroos. I mean, who thinks kangaroos are scary?"

He gave Ryan a superior look. "And they *did* keep the humans in cages, and they used them for slaves and pack animals. Yeah, that's right. And they didn't live in a Lifespring—they lived down in a spooky old mine."

"But with no Rooz," said Chucky sadly, "it's just not the same story. I like the way Ryan tells it."

Brad stared at the chubby teenager. "I hope you're not saying that *he* can tell a story better than *me*?"

"Mine isn't a story," said Ryan softly. Now everyone looked at him again.

Brad grinned. "Are you trying to tell us that you really went to this weird place?"

Ryan shrugged. "I've been telling people that since the beginning, but they won't believe me."

Tracy shifted her feet and stared down at the ground, embarrassed for him. He wanted to tell her that *they* were the ones who were wrong, but he knew that she didn't believe him either. Maybe he had been wrong to tell any of them.

"Ryan just says that to make it more interesting," said Chucky. "Tell them the truth, Ry—Tao isn't a real place."

"But it is. Tao *is* a real place."

Brad roared with laughter. "Man, I think you got hit in the head with too many footballs. Does the coach

8

know about this? Maybe we ought to tell him that the water boy sees imaginary lands and killer kangaroos."

"*Kung fu* kangaroos," Chucky corrected him.

"Excuse me," said Brad, "kung fu kangaroos. Tell me, Ryan, how to get to this land? Do you just snap your fingers, or do you have to say some magic words?"

"Leave him alone," muttered Tracy.

"It's okay," said Ryan. "I used the Manuscript to get there, but I'm not sure how it works."

With a smirk on his face, Brad lifted his hands. "Buddy, if you can get to this place, it can't be too difficult. You probably just say 'abracadabra,' and snap your fingers."

To demonstrate, Brad snapped his fingers.

And everything went strangely, eerily silent.

They all looked at one another, but no one seemed able to find a voice. Suddenly, in the distance, Ryan heard a slow, sliding slither, as if a thousand whispers were rasping toward them. Blades of grass seemed to bow to him in a great, rolling wave, bending their backs to the wind that had come out of nowhere at the far end of the field.

Ryan had the strangest feeling, as if this had happened to him once before. Then he suddenly realized what it reminded him of, and he shivered. The first time he'd gone to Tao, his journey had started with a churning torrent of water. The sound of that flood rushing toward him was unforgettable, and he never thought he'd hear it again. But he was wrong: the sound of the water was also the sound of the wind racing toward them. Ryan blinked, and turned away for a moment.

As he did, the wind reached them, and roared around them, blowing so strongly they had to lean into it to keep from falling back. Carried on the wind was a season's worth of fallen leaves, swirling flocks of red and yellow and orange. Ryan looked up in time to catch a glimpse of Tracy's frightened face before the wild cloud of leaves swept around them, and then his entire world was blown away in a rustling, crackling confusion.

chapter
2

RYAN MATERIALIZED NEAR HIS FRIENDS IN a bizarre-looking woods with dark green tree trunks reaching so high that he couldn't see the tops. The branches were covered with glimmering blue moss. There were strange, chittering sounds all around them, and a few autumn leaves fluttered down.

The five kids stood huddled in fright until Brad spotted Ryan. He grabbed the smaller boy by the collar and shook him. "Okay, you had better get us out of here right now!"

Ryan had never seen Brad look so scared. "Listen, you did it the right way . . . just snap your fingers."

"Yeah, yeah!" said Brad. Frantically, he snapped his fingers, muttering, "Abracadabra! Abracadabra!"

Chucky made a little squeaking sound and pointed into the lush forest. "Nnyyaah . . . nnyyaah—"

11

"No, those aren't the right words," said Brad. "It's abracadabra-a-a-a-a . . ." His voice trailed off as he saw what Chucky was looking at.

A giant creature, looking a little like a kangaroo, stood before them in the forest. He was wearing a wooden vest and green clothing, and he carried a long wooden staff. Suddenly the Roo leaped into the air and landed in front of them, swishing his tail back and forth.

The visitors gasped and stumbled backward, except for Ryan, who grinned.

Brad sunk to his knees and begged, "Don't hurt us! Please, don't hurt us!"

"I thought kangaroos weren't s-s-scary," said Toby, his teeth chattering.

The Roo scratched the white fur under his chin and studied their faces. "Ryan?"

"Lai!" called the boy. He shouldered his way past the others and stood before the Master of Wood. "Then it's true? We're really here!"

"Yes, Newcomer, you're really here." He pointed his staff at Brad. "Arise. There's no need to be afraid of us."

Brad bristled and jumped to his feet. "I wasn't afraid! You just startled me, that's all."

The towering Warrior made a bow to his visitors. "Welcome to Tao. My name is Lai, and I follow the

12

virtue of Order. I am a disciple of the Shaolin fighting style. We weren't sure exactly where you would arrive, so we've been searching the forest for you. Allow me to summon the others."

Lai lifted a wood flute from a cord around his neck and blew it, making a shrill sound that pierced the dark forest. Birds fluttered from the trees and shot off in all directions, screeching loudly.

Ryan was amazed at all the plants growing around them. He remembered most of Tao being black and ruined, except for the Radius of Green. With everything fresh and growing, it seemed like spring. Ryan wondered if it could be fall in his world and spring in Tao.

Suddenly the ground began to tremble. Everyone looked worriedly at Ryan, but he could only grin. He was thrilled just to be back in this enchanted land, and this time he had *witnesses*. But his witnesses looked as if they wanted to burrow into the ground and hide.

The thudding grew more intense, and it felt as if a great herd was running toward them. The leaves rustled, and four figures flashed through the air and landed in the clearing. The Newcomers gasped as they were surrounded by long-tailed, long-eared creatures, dressed in colorful robes and sashes.

Tracy stared wide-eyed at Ryan, and he gave her a wink.

"Cool!" gushed Chucky. He pointed at the biggest one of them all, a Roo with metal rings hanging across his massive chest. "Yee, right?"

The big Roo nodded solemnly.

Ryan whispered to Chucky. "Remember, he doesn't talk."

"Oh yeah. What does he do?"

"The secret handshake." Ryan ran up to Yee, and they bumped hips and did a complicated handshake, ending with their arms crisscrossed. Yee and Ryan laughed, while the other kids just stared at them.

"Ryan! How good to see you." A regal, Roo stepped forward. He was wearing a blue tunic and sash, and a long, crystalline sword hung from his belt.

"Yun!" said Ryan. "It's good to see you too. And I haven't forgotten a thing. Ever since I left here, I've been living with virtue."

Yun smiled slightly. "Yes, I see you have been telling your friends about us. That is good, because we haven't got much time."

"Wait a minute," said Brad with a scowl. "Do you mind telling us why you brought us here?"

"Not at all," answered Yun. "You have been brought here because Tao needs you. Just as Tao needed Ryan during the war with Komodo. Just as Tao needed Master Chung. But I'm getting ahead of myself; introductions are necessary first. I am Yun, and my virtue is Benevolence. I try not to fight, but when I must, I use the Tai Chi style. I am the Master of Water."

He pointed to the Roo in the wooden armor. "You have met Lai, whose virtue is Order. His element is wood."

Next he moved to the biggest Roo. "You also seem to know Yee, whose virtue is Righteousness. He uses the Hung Chuan style and the metal rings. He is the Master of Metal."

Then Yun motioned to the Roo with the prettiest features and the biggest sword. "This is Tsun, whose virtue is Loyalty. Her fighting style is Wing Chun, which uses an opponent's own strength against him. She is the Master of Earth." The fair Roo nodded to the visitors.

The last Warrior of Virtue stood at attention, holding a spear. The fringe on his sash was bright red—so bright that it looked as if his clothes were on fire.

"This is Chi," said Yun. "His virtue is Wisdom, and his style of combat is Choi Lee Fut. He uses the flaming whips, and he's Master of Fire."

Chucky grinned. "Pleased to meet you. I'm Chucky, the Master of Food Fights. My weapon is the spoonful of mashed potatoes."

The Rooz nodded, looking very impressed.

Ryan frowned. "Let me do the introductions, okay? This is Tracy. She's really smart and gets good grades in school."

"That is wise," said Chi.

Ryan went on, "You met Chucky. I guess he *is* the Master of Food Fights. And this is Brad, the Master of, uh . . . Football."

"And Basketball too," added Brad.

"And this is Toby—"

The big fullback reached out a hand to Lai. "When I get in a fight, I usually use a bear hug. What do you call that?"

"Foolish," said Lai. "Unless you are a bear."

"Later there will be time to discuss martial arts," said Yun. "Right now, we must tell them why the power of Tao brought them here."

"Yeah, what's the deal?" grumbled Brad.

Yun pointed to some fallen tree trunks, and the Newcomers sat down to listen. "I am sure Ryan must have told you about our enemy, Komodo. He had an iron grip over all of the Lifesprings on Tao, and he almost destroyed them to steal the Zubrium."

Brad and Toby had some questions about Zubrium, and Yun answered them. He ended by saying, "With Ryan's help, we defeated Komodo and freed the land of Tao."

The big Roo gave Ryan a smile, and the boy beamed proudly.

"Lifesprings all across Tao have come back to health," said Yun. "The Zubrium is flowing again.

Yun and the Sea Serpent

Many Warmbloods and humans have returned to live in the Lifesprings, but they got used to Komodo running their lives. Without him, they don't know what to do about the new problems they face."

Yun sighed. "So each of us must return home to the Lifespring where we were born—to set things straight. Since having Ryan along last time brought us such good luck, we decided that each of us would take a Newcomer as a traveling companion. That way, each can learn the wisdom of the other."

"Wait a minute," said Tracy. "I've got homework to do, and a test tomorrow."

"And we've got a big game on Friday," said Brad.

Yun held up his paw. "When you return to your world, only a few moments will have passed."

The Newcomers looked at one another with relief, and Chucky grinned. "That sounds all right."

"That is, if you're still alive," added Lai.

The smile faded from Chucky's face. "What do you mean by that?"

"Simple logic," answered Lai. "If you're dead, you can't very well return home."

"On second thought—" said Toby with a gulp.

"Come on," urged Ryan, "this will be the adventure of a lifetime! The Warriors of Virtue wouldn't ask for our help unless they needed it. You aren't afraid, are you?"

"No way," said Toby. "Count me in!"

"I like your spirit," said Lai to the big fullback. "Would you like to come with me to the Emerald Lifespring?"

"Sure."

Tsun walked up to Tracy and said, "The Wing Chun fighting style was first taught by a woman, and I would like to teach you. Will you come with me to the Mushroom Lifespring?"

Tracy nodded hesitantly. "If Ryan says we should help you, then we should."

Yee pointed to Brad and crossed his arms. It was as if the silent Warrior had chosen the Newcomer with the biggest mouth. He was a brave Roo, thought Ryan.

"Okay," muttered Brad, "I'll go."

Chi stepped beside Chucky and said, "I will take the Master of the Food Fight to the Volcano Lifespring."

"Lead on," said Chucky, sounding more brave than he looked.

Ryan glanced at Yun and shrugged. "I guess that leaves me with you."

"As I wished," said Yun with a bow. "Tao will benefit from your wisdom."

"I hope so," said Ryan. He looked around at his fellow Newcomers from the land of car pools and TV dinners. They had stunned looks on their faces, as if they thought they were dreaming. He didn't blame them, because on his first trip to Tao, he couldn't believe it either.

But when people started chasing him and trying to hurt him, it quickly sunk in. This was real. He hoped his friends would be all right.

"After we are finished with our tasks," said Yun, "we shall meet at Master Chung's Lifespring." He glanced at Ryan. "We have renamed it in his honor."

"Master Chung deserved it," agreed Ryan.

Yun looked gratefully into the faces of the Newcomers. "Thank you for helping us. May virtue be yours."

They started walking off in different directions, Chucky with Chi, Tsun and Tracy, and Lai and Toby. Even Brad seemed impressed to be walking alongside the stoic Yee.

Ryan looked up at Yun and could hardly believe this was happening to him again. Although he knew that Tao could be beautiful, it could also be dangerous.

"Listen, you guys!" he called to his friends. "Look out for yourselves!"

"No problem!" answered Chucky as he chased after his long-tailed companion. The young humans and the big Warmbloods soon disappeared into the towering forest.

Ryan had to run so fast to keep up with Yun's big hops that he barely had time to breathe, let alone talk.

Finally the Warrior of Virtue stopped beside a stream about six feet wide, and bent down to get a cooling drink. For the first time, Ryan noticed that Yun's sword glowed slightly when water was near.

The boy staggered up behind him, panting. "Can we . . . can we rest a second?"

"Yes," answered Yun. "I'm sorry to make us hurry, but we have a long journey ahead of us. Please drink some water, and rest for a moment."

Gratefully, Ryan got down on his hands and knees and crawled across the soft moss to the edge of the rushing water. He watched the Roo bend over and drink from the stream as if it was a big drinking fountain, and the boy tried to do the same thing.

But Ryan didn't have Yun's long neck and snout, so he had to bend way over the swirling water to get a drink. As he did, his hands slipped on the wet moss. With a shout of surprise, the boy tumbled head-first into the water.

The stream was deeper than it looked, and it was cold and swift. Ryan bobbed to the surface and sputtered, "Help! Help!"

Something long and thick wrapped around his waist— it felt like a giant snake! Ryan struggled against the thick tentacle, but he sunk deeper and deeper. Freezing water rushed into his mouth and nose.

Oh, no! thought Ryan. *The first day of my new adventure in Tao, and I'm going to drown!*

chapter
3

SUDDENLY, THE SNAKE AROUND HIS MID-dle jerked him out of the stream and dropped him onto the bank. As Ryan shook the water off his face, he realized that it wasn't a snake at all—it was Yun's tail!

"You saved me with your tail," he said in amazement.

Yun nodded. "A tail is a very useful appendage. You never waste movement if you have a tail." The Roo unwrapped a thick blue sash from his waist and draped it around the boy's shoulders. "I'm sorry."

"Why are you sorry?" asked Ryan, shivering.

"It's my fault you fell in, for not allowing us enough time to rest."

"N-No," insisted Ryan through chattering teeth. "I'm just . . . clumsy."

"Good balance is very important," said Yun. "You

21

needed better balance when you leaned over the stream to drink. I needed to balance our exercise with more rest. As a student of Tai Chi, I should know better."

Ryan shivered as a stiff breeze swirled around him. He hadn't noticed the breeze before—but in his wet condition, it felt like a hurricane. The leaves rustled overhead, but the sunshine couldn't break through. On the floor of the dense forest, it was dark . . . and cold.

"I must get you to shelter," said Yun. The big Roo leaped a few times into the air, as if he was trying to scan above the treetops. Although he never got that high, he got a good view. "There's a mountain to the north of us," he announced.

Without another word, Yun picked up Ryan and sped away on his powerful hind legs. The boy tried to protest, but he was shivering too much to talk. He knew he had to get out of the wind, and his wet clothes.

Crunching branches and leaves under his big feet, Yun headed uphill to the base of the mountain. He set Ryan down on a bed of pine needles and began to poke through the bushes.

"W-What are you doing?" asked Ryan.

"Looking for a cave. Ah, here's one." He pointed to a small opening about two feet wide.

Hunched with cold, Ryan staggered over to the entrance of the cave. It smelled like wet fur and bacon grease inside the dark hole, and he scrunched up his face. He didn't really want to go in there, but he didn't want to freeze to death either.

"Take off your clothes," ordered Yun. "I will dry them."

Ryan shrugged. "If you say so."

A few minutes later, Ryan was sitting inside the cave. He wasn't naked, because he had several of Yun's robes wrapped around him. He watched silently as Yun took each article of sopping clothing between his paws, and concentrated. Although Ryan knew what to expect, he was still impressed. Water streamed from the cloth, creating a pattering sound as it dribbled onto the rocks below, as a dry spot formed in the center of the fabric and spread out, like a stain in reverse. He had almost forgotten that water was the Roo's element.

The big Roo sat at the entrance of the cave, shaking his head. "My fault."

"No," said Ryan, "you blame yourself too much." If Yun had a fault, it was that he took it personally when anything went wrong.

"As a student of Tai Chi, I should know when our balance is off. In my haste to reach the Lifespring, I made us rush too fast, without enough rest."

"What is your home Lifespring called?" asked Ryan, trying to change the subject.

"The Lagoon Lifespring." Yun looked wistful for a

moment. "I haven't seen it since I was a young Warmblood. It's on an island, in the middle of the Jade Sea. I remember it as being very beautiful."

He looked down. "When Komodo conquered the Lagoon Lifespring, we were forced to flee. I have never returned, because I didn't want to see it in ruins. With my love for water, I take the memory of my home with me wherever I go."

"Why are we going there now?" asked Ryan. "What kind of problems could they have in such a beautiful place?"

"Reports are sketchy," said Yun.

"But you must have heard something."

The big Roo looked off into the distance, staring hard at nothing. "The Jade Sea is part of the Azure Chain, a series of small inland seas that were formed when an earthquake breached an underground ocean, flooding the surface world. The seas are very deep, and hold many secrets." He paused, and then looked at Ryan. "The Lagoon Lifespring is being threatened by one of those secrets. A sea serpent."

The boy stared. "A sea serpent?"

"Yes. Where you have a sea, you usually have a sea serpent. Isn't it that way where you come from?"

Ryan shook his head. "No, we haven't had any trouble with sea serpents in a while."

"You're lucky."

Yun and the Sea Serpent

The boy looked doubtful. "What are we going to do when we, uh, meet this sea serpent?"

"I don't know," answered Yun. "But thanks to you, we're not going to walk there."

"We're not?"

"No." The Roo suddenly jumped to his feet and stood on one foot like a stork, with his other foot sticking out at an odd angle. Despite this awkward stance, Yun held perfectly still. In fact, he looked like a statue.

"Tai Chi teaches that there should be no wasted movement," said Yun. "The first masters of Tai Chi learned from watching cranes and turtles, who save their energy until they need it. They also watched the reeds on the lake which bend with the wind. From this, they learned to be *soft* when taking a blow."

His paws and feet flashed with lightning speed, and Yun was suddenly frozen again, standing on the other leg. "But the masters also learned to be *hard* when striking a blow. Water is a perfect teacher of Tai Chi. When you strike water, it is soft—you can't hurt it. But when the water wishes to strike you, it rises up as a great wave and is very hard."

Yun moved slowly and gracefully through several poses, like a dancer. "This balance is important in all things. Master Chung called it the Yin and the Yang."

"I've heard of that," said Ryan. "Like how a positive charge is attracted to a negative charge."

"Exactly. Good and bad, day and night, sweet and sour—you must have both."

Ryan shook his head puzzledly. "I still don't see how that will save us from walking through the forest."

Yun bowed to his young companion. "You showed me the way when you fell into the stream. Even when you are clumsy, Ryan, you are wise. If we try to walk to the sea, you will never keep up with me, and I can't carry you that far. However, as you demonstrated, the *water* can carry you."

His arms moved like waves. "The water can carry us both, because water always flows to the sea. We'll build a raft, put it in the stream, and float to the sea with the least amount of effort. This is the Tai Chi and the way of water. Thank you for reminding me."

"You're welcome," said Ryan with a yawn. "Always glad to be of help."

Yun drew his crystalline sword. For a moment, it rippled like a stream of water, before hardening again.

I'm seeing things, thought Ryan. *I must be tired.*

"Why don't you sleep while I cut fallen logs and vines for the raft?" said Yun kindly.

Although the cave was filthy and smelled of wet fur, Ryan's body didn't care. More than anything, he just wanted to stretch out and close his eyes. He pulled

Yun's robes tighter around him and lay down. "Maybe, just for a minute."

Within a few seconds, the Newcomer was asleep.

As he slept in the smelly old cave, Ryan had a surprisingly pleasant dream. He was at home on a lazy Saturday afternoon, just hanging around the house. He read a book, played catch with his dad and painted a model airplane. It was one of those relaxed days when there wasn't anything to do but be alive.

Later in the afternoon, Ryan went for a walk with his dog, Bravo. He kept the golden retriever on a leash until they reached the park, then he set him free. Ryan wasn't really supposed to let Bravo run loose in the park, but it didn't seem to matter.

That was when he began to suspect it was a dream.

Bravo bounded all over the place, in and out of the trees, and through the streams. As he frolicked, he seemed to get bigger—several times he stood upright and walked like a human. With a start, Ryan realized that his golden retriever had turned into a Warmblood!

Ryan felt his own tongue hanging out of the side of his mouth, which was unusual. He reached up to touch his face—and got a glimpse of his arm. It was covered with fur, and he had a paw! Now he reached anxiously for his face and found a fur-covered muzzle, long teeth and a cold nose. When he tried to shout in alarm, it came out "Woof!"

Yikes! He had turned into a Warmblood too!

Bravo strode up to him, walking upright. "Hey, Ryan," he said in a gruff voice, "let's go! There are squirrels over there we could chase."

Ryan caught sight of his own tail, and he pushed it behind him. "What's going on? What's happening to us? Why did we turn into Warmbloods?"

"Quit fooling around," barked Bravo. "Let's go play!" With long strides, he loped off into the trees.

Ryan bounced around on his hind legs, anxious to chase his friend. Then he barked, and the sound shocked him. *Get a grip!* he told himself. He liked dogs, but he didn't want to *be* one. Also he didn't feel comfortable chasing squirrels, even if the idea did make him drool.

This dream had been okay, but now it had taken a strange turn. With reluctance, Ryan dragged himself awake, and he watched the park swirl into the distance. At once, pungent smells attacked his nose, and he felt clammy darkness all around him.

The closeness of the cave was stifling, and Ryan had to get out. He tossed off his robes and scurried out the narrow hole into the open. To his surprise, it was twilight, and long shadows stretched across the cloud-shrouded mountain. Ryan could see a pile of logs and vines on the ground, and he figured Yun was nearby.

A moment later, he heard Yun's big feet shuffling through the forest, and he waited patiently. Even though Ryan was naked, he wasn't cold.

With one hop, the big Roo bounded into the clearing. He carried at least a dozen logs in his arms, and some were as tall as he was. He didn't see Ryan until he dropped the logs and looked up. His soft brown eyes widened in shock.

"Oh my goodness!" gasped Yun.

"What?" asked Ryan. He looked around, and once again he caught sight of his tail. "Oh no!"

With mounting dread, Ryan stared down at his body. Just as before in his dream, he was covered with reddish-brown fur! He touched his face and found a cold nose, a long muzzle and sharp canine teeth. He pushed his hands higher and found two floppy ears!

Desperately he rubbed his eyes. "I need to wake up! Why can't I wake up?"

"You're awake, Ryan," said Yun softly. "That must have been an enchanted cave."

"An enchanted cave!" howled Ryan. "Woof! Woof! Why didn't you warn me? Woof!"

"I didn't know," said Yun with a helpless shrug. "I thought Komodo destroyed all the enchanted caves.

They must be coming back to life, along with the forest."

It seemed to Ryan as if Yun was trying not to smile. The Roo pulled a pile of clothes out of his pouch. "Your clothes are dry."

"Great!" barked Ryan, leaping around. "My clothes are dry, but I don't *need* clothes anymore!" His jaws tightened, and his sharp teeth clacked together. "I'm trying hard not to growl at you, Yun."

"You could growl at me," said the Roo, "but it wouldn't help."

Ryan started leaping around on all fours, howling and growling. How had he gotten into this mess? The new Warmblood stopped for a moment, scratched behind a floppy ear and came up with an idea.

"I know, I'll go back into the cave! That will make me human again." On all four legs, he scrambled into the cave. A moment later, Ryan was sitting cross-legged in the exact spot where he had fallen asleep. "Okay, I'm ready."

"I wouldn't count on that working," said Yun, crouching by the entrance of the cave. "An enchanted cave usually only works in one direction."

"Enchanted caves! Whoever heard of such a thing? You ought to put warning signs on these."

"We did, but Komodo took them all down. I'm sorry,

Yun and the Sea Serpent

Ryan, I didn't know we had to worry about enchanted caves. It means that Tao is getting back to normal."

"Well, that's great. Tao is back to normal, but I look like my dog's big brother!" Ryan refused to believe any of this. How could he go back to his regular life looking like this? For his birthday, Tracy would probably get him a flea collar.

"This isn't fair!" grumbled Ryan. "I was just getting used to being human."

"You stay in the cave," said Yun, "and I'll start putting the raft together. We can set out on the stream tomorrow morning. If you're hungry, how about some rice cakes?"

"How about a rabbit?" snapped Ryan. He blinked in amazement, surprised at his own words.

"Now, now," said Yun, "you have to curb those instincts. Warmbloods don't kill, and humans shouldn't either. Maybe you'd *like* a rabbit, but you're going to have some rice cakes."

He opened his pouch and began to take out cakes wrapped in bright green leaves. As Yun unpacked their provisions, Ryan crossed his arms and scowled. He had a tail, but it sure wasn't wagging.

"Yun?" he asked. "Is this how Warmbloods came to be? People and animals went into these enchanted caves—and somehow turned into Warmbloods?"

The Roo shrugged. "I don't know. Warmbloods have

been in Tao ever since I can remember, and so have enchanted caves. Some of them turn males to females, or they make people fall in love with the first person they see. You never know." He frowned. "You don't have enchanted caves in your world?"

"No!" growled Ryan. "And we don't have sea serpents, Lifesprings, dragons, and . . . and . . ."

"And Warmbloods," said Yun, finishing his sentence. "You don't have Warmbloods either."

"No," muttered Ryan. "If I can't change back to human, I'll have to stay here."

"There are worse places than Tao," said Yun, unwrapping a rice cake. "Although when you came here the first time, things were pretty bad. Want a rice cake?"

Ryan shook his head, and his ears flapped back and forth. "Tao is the coolest place I've ever seen, and I learned a lot here. But this isn't my home. I've got my parents and friends, and there are things I want to do, like take Tracy to a dance. Do you think she'll go with me if I look like this?"

"You do have a problem," agreed Yun. "I can't imagine a place without Warmbloods. How strange." He opened his fire-starting kit. "Would you like a fire to keep warm?"

"No! I'm burning up in all this fur."

"Try not to fight it, Ryan," said the Warrior of

Virtue. "Remember, it's best to bend with the wind. Be soft."

"I'm so soft I feel like a teddy bear!" growled Ryan. "No offense, Yun, but this didn't happen to you. It happened to *me*! How would you like it, if you suddenly became human?"

Yun smiled. "Some of my best friends are human."

"I don't see anything funny about it." Ryan turned his back to the Roo and stared into the darkness of the cave.

He heard Yun sigh. "Well, I think I'll build a fire to give myself some light. I've got plenty of old, dried wood, and I can't use all of it for the raft. You rest, Ryan."

Rest? *Sure.* With a growl, Ryan lay down in the smelly, greasy cave and tried to go to sleep, but fear and worry gnawed at his stomach, making him feel sick. What if sleeping in the cave again didn't work? What if he couldn't find a way to change back?

He supposed he could grow up to be like the Warriors of Virtue. That wouldn't be so bad. But he would never be as big and strong as they were. Besides, he was probably the only golden retriever Warmblood in all of Tao!

After sulking for a while, Ryan turned over and gazed out the mouth of the cave. By the flickering firelight, he watched Yun trim the logs for the raft.

With great care and patience, he tied the logs together, and the raft began to take shape.

It looked like a fine vessel. Ryan could tell that Yun loved boats, or anything to do with water.

Several times, the Roo looked up to see Ryan watching him, but he never said anything. What could he say? *Be soft.* Ryan was going to be soft tonight— and stay in the cave—because he had no choice. If the curse wasn't gone by morning, he would be howling mad.

Gazing at the glow of the campfire, Ryan finally fell asleep. He wanted to dream about being human, but instead he and Bravo spent the night chasing squirrels through the park.

chapter
4

AS THE SUN ROSE OVER TAO, A SLIVER OF daylight crawled down the mountainside. It stretched across the rocks and slipped into the mouth of the cave. Finally, the light raced across the grimy earthen floor and settled on Ryan's eyelids.

He sat up, and he didn't know where he was—except that it was dark, clammy and smelled like a dog pound. Then Ryan remembered what had happened to him. When he reached behind his back and grabbed a bushy tail, his howls could be heard all over Tao.

"Please calm down," said Yun. The Roo was sitting outside the cave, using a slender brush to paint on a chunk of wood. "I told you it probably wouldn't work. What good would an enchanted cave be if you could switch right back?"

Ryan charged out of the cave and bounded around

on all four legs, until he remembered that he could stand upright. He jumped to his feet and wailed, "You've got to do something to help me! Yun, please, get me out of this!"

"If I knew how to end it," said Yun, "I would do so. Maybe the elders at the Lagoon Lifespring will be able to help you."

"Are we still going there?" asked Ryan nervously. "I'm not sure I want to . . . now."

Yun finished painting and wiped off his brush with a leaf. "You know what, Ryan, you're pretty good at feeling sorry for yourself."

"Hey, I didn't ask for this to happen! I didn't deserve it."

The Roo looked at him with intense but kindly eyes. "Do you remember when we first met? I was alone, hiding from the other Warriors of Virtue."

"Yes, I remember," answered Ryan. "What does that have to do with the enchanted cave?"

"I was hiding because I had killed a man. I didn't ask for him to attack me, and I didn't want to kill him. But it happened, just like you falling asleep in the cave. Because of that, I shut myself off from other people for a long time. You were the one who told me I was wrong."

Ryan frowned. "This is different."

"Is it?" The Roo kept painting. "Life is always

changing, like the wind and the ocean. Don't shut yourself off because you make a mistake. No matter what happens in your life, other people still need you. The people at the Lagoon Lifespring need our help badly."

"But . . . will people accept me like this?"

The big Roo smiled. "Believe me, you'll be accepted wherever we go. People won't know you're a Newcomer anymore. You look like a Warmblood, so be a Warmblood."

Ryan scratched behind a floppy ear. "I hadn't thought of that. It might be interesting, just to blend in."

"One more thing," said Yun, "do you still have your limp?"

Ryan took a few steps. "No, I don't. Okay, there are some good parts to this thing, but I'd like to be human again. No offense."

"None taken." Yun picked up the chunk of wood and turned it around so that Ryan could see what he had painted. Ryan had thought it was a picture, but instead it was a sign with two words on it: "Beware! Enchanted!"

He pounded the sign into the dirt in front of the cave. "Now we can go."

Ryan scratched the fur on his stomach and thought about life. Yun was right about one thing. Life kept changing, and you had to go with the flow, or go crazy.

"Can I have my clothes now?" asked Ryan.

"Sure," said Yun with a smile. He tossed the young Warmblood his shirt, pants and jacket. Ryan struggled to put the clothes on; they were tight. They had to fit over his fur.

When they were ready to go, Yun picked up the raft, which was about four feet wide and eight feet long.

"Need any help?" asked Ryan.

"No," answered the Roo. "The water is going to do most of the work."

As sunlight filtered through the trees, they left the mountain and walked through the forest. It was a short trip to the stream where Ryan had fallen in, and he stopped to look into the dark, swirling water. It was funny how a small act, like falling into a stream, could cause such big problems.

Now they were going back into the water on purpose, which was probably crazy. For some reason, Ryan didn't feel afraid. Maybe it was because he was with Yun, who was always calm and brave. But it wasn't only Yun. Ryan felt strong and confident, as if he could fight a whole fleet of sea serpents.

He looked down at his furry arms and wondered if his new confidence was part of being a Warmblood. Humans often thought and worried too much. Sometimes it was better to take action and worry about it later, like wild animals did. Warmbloods were hardly wild animals, but there was some wildness left in them. Ryan could feel it.

He glanced over to see Yun checking his raft. It looked sturdy enough to float all the way to China.

"Ready?" asked Yun with a smile.

"Let's go!" said Ryan.

Yun lowered the raft into the moving current and let go of it. Ryan gasped, thinking it would float away, but Yun held the end of the raft with his tail. Ryan wagged his own tail, wondering if there was anything useful he could do with it.

"Get in front," ordered Yun.

Since the raft was almost as wide as the stream, Ryan only had to climb over a few inches of water. He eased onto the raft and dug his long fingernails into the wood. Being a Warmblood, he had good balance, and he barely got wet. Not only that, but his sleek fur acted like a wet suit, keeping his skin dry.

Hey, this isn't so bad, thought Ryan. Maybe he could be the first Warmblood quarterback on the school football team.

Suddenly, the raft plunged into the water, as Yun climbed aboard. The current caught the craft, and it took off like a race car, shooting down the stream.

Ryan kept his head above the spray and shook his fur. He hardly had time to yell a warning before they crashed into a mass of roots growing from the bank. Ryan almost fell off, but he dug his long nails into the wood and hung on.

He glanced back at Yun and growled.

"I never said you wouldn't get wet," answered the Roo. He drew his sword and stuck the long, blue blade into the water. "Let me see if I can steer us."

At once, the passage became smoother, and they cruised down the middle of the waterway. "It'll get wider as we get closer to the ocean," said Yun.

"Yeah," answered Ryan, trying to shake the water off his face. Now that they were drifting with the current in the stream's center, it felt as if the raft was holding still and the forest was rushing past them.

Ryan finally had to stop looking at the bank, because it was making him dizzy. At least he wasn't cold anymore, and it would only get warmer as the day went on.

"Look out for rapids," said Yun.

"Rapids?" yelped Ryan.

"Or there may not be any rapids," said Yun. "But I've never ridden this stream before."

"Great," said Ryan.

They drifted for almost an hour. Another stream joined theirs, making it several feet wider and much faster. This only made Ryan worry more about rapids. He was so intent on looking for white water that he didn't see the black tangle of thorns and driftwood—until they hit it.

The raft plowed into the barrier, and Ryan's fur got snagged in the thorns. He tried to twist his way out, but it only got worse.

"Help!" he cried.

"Close your eyes!" Yun swung his mighty sword over his head and slammed it into the tangle. With a crunch, the thorns splintered, and the raft lurched ahead. Ryan was supposed to keep his eyes shut, but he had to watch Yun hack his way through the thicket. With two more blows of his crystal sword, they were free.

Once again, they drifted lazily down the stream, which was now about ten feet wide. Ryan picked the burrs and thorns from his fur, while he kept watch for rapids and more snags.

"You're sure this way is quicker?" he asked doubt-fully.

"Oh yes," answered Yun. "We've gone many miles, and it would have taken us much longer to walk. In the forest, there would be even more thickets to chop our way through."

"I suppose," said Ryan with a sigh.

The Roo smiled. "Maybe we should stop to eat soon. What do you think?"

"Sure," answered Ryan. "And I wouldn't mind a good shake to get the water off."

A short time later, the stream flowed into a rugged canyon, and rock walls rose on either side of them. The dark green trees of the forest thinned and gave way to groups of yellow trees, which dipped their branches into the water and left trails of pink flower petals.

After floating for hours through the forest, it seemed strange to leave the dark canopy of trees. In its own way, the canyon was just as beautiful. Millions of years of erosion and history were visible in the grooves and streaks on the rock walls.

Ryan was also grateful for the warmth of the sun on his hairy back.

The stream widened into a series of small terraces and waterfalls, which were scattered across the canyon floor like magical steps. As the water flowed over the waterfalls, it collected in shallow pools. Ryan gazed into a pool and saw sparkling green lights at the bottom. The green lights turned the water a beautiful turquoise color.

"There is coral in these pools collecting Zubrium," said Yun. "I'm afraid we'll damage them. Let's get out and portage the raft to the other side."

With his sword, Yun guided the raft toward the sandy bank, and Ryan jumped out and pulled it ashore. Even after floating for hours in an icy stream, he still felt strong and healthy. He pulled off his wet clothes and shook himself like a dog.

Yun laughed at him. "Are you sure you were never a Warmblood before?"

Ryan smiled. "No, but I've been friends with a lot of dogs."

Carefully, they carried the raft around the stretch of tiny waterfalls. Before they put it back into the stream, Yun opened his pouch and took out some rice cakes. Ryan figured the cakes would be ruined from the water, but the oily leaves had kept them dry.

They ate in silence, watching the stream flow from one shining pool to another. They weren't alone either; a flock of scarlet birds had come to bathe in the turquoise water. Ryan decided that he had never seen any place as beautiful as these gentle waterfalls.

"You've never seen this place?" he asked Yun.

The Roo shook his head. "No, I haven't. When Komodo ruled Tao, this land was dead and brown, and the water was polluted. Now it has come back to life. If the coral keeps growing and collecting Zubrium, one day there will be a new Lifespring right here."

"I'd like to come back to see that," said Ryan.

"That could be in a million years or more."

"It takes that long for a Lifespring to grow?" asked Ryan with surprise.

"Yes. But it only takes a moment to destroy one."

Yun looked sad as he gazed at the aquamarine pools. "All of life is that way—years to grow and only a second to die. That's why you must never take a life. The life of even one person is even more precious than a Lifespring, because you can never bring a person back to life."

"What about an enemy?" asked Ryan. "A bad guy."

"Especially an enemy. To be kind to an enemy is the highest virtue."

Ryan looked puzzled. "Then why do you learn to fight?"

"Because," said Yun with a sigh, "not everyone lives with virtue, as we do. All of us have good and evil inside, and some of us give in to the evil.

"The Warriors of Virtue are sworn to protect innocent people from those who would harm them, and we do. But there is a time to fight, and a time to make peace. The time to make peace is always at hand. Remember that, Ryan."

The Newcomer nodded, rose to his feet and stretched. "It feels good to be dry again. Are you sure we can't walk to the ocean?"

"No, my friend," answered Yun, putting their scraps of food back into his pack. "You picked a swift current for our journey, and that was the right choice. This stream will soon become a mighty river."

"That's what I'm afraid of," said Ryan with a gulp.

Yun and the Sea Serpent

The Roo stared past him into the sky, and his smile turned into a frown. He jumped to his feet and drew his sword.

"What is it?" asked Ryan. He followed Yun's gaze and saw a bird flying down the middle of the canyon, headed straight toward them. It didn't look much different from the other birds in the canyon, until Ryan realized how far away it was.

"Wow," he said. "That's a big bird."

"*If* it's a bird," answered Yun.

Ryan stared. "What else could it be?"

"Maybe it's a great white crane," said Yun, not sounding convinced.

"What else *bad* could it be?" asked Ryan.

Yun lifted his sword. "We'll know soon. I would tell you to hide, but it's already seen us. So stand behind me."

Ryan scurried behind the big Roo and watched the sky. The creature flapped its wings in a lazy fashion. It didn't seem to be in any hurry, but it was clearly flying straight toward them.

chapter 5

THE GIANT BIRD SAILED OVER THE CANYON and dropped into a slow descent. Ryan could see its odd silhouette against the blue sky. It looked almost like a swan in the front, with a long, graceful neck. Yet it had an ugly beak, and four legs, like a horse. And it seemed to have armor on its back, like a turtle. Ryan rubbed his eyes.

When he opened his eyes again, the fantastic creature had drawn close enough to show its colorful feathers. Maybe it was a bird after all, thought Ryan. Its plumage came in five brilliant colors—black, white, red, green and yellow—but it had striped fur like a zebra. What kind of animal was it?

Ryan leaned around to look at Yun, and he wished he hadn't. The Roo looked very worried. "It's a

Hoggarth," he whispered. "Master Chung also called it a Phoenix."

"A Phoenix!" gasped Ryan. He thought they were mythical beings. Well, they were mythical, except on Tao.

He gulped. "Is it, like, going to eat us?"

"Maybe. Some Hoggarth are good, but some aren't. They are magical creatures, very powerful and unpredictable."

Ryan looked around for someplace to hide, but this wasn't a dense forest. There was nothing but sheer rock and turquoise water all around them.

"Stay behind me," ordered Yun. As the creature circled for a landing, the Roo lifted his sword even higher.

A magical creature, thought Ryan. *Could it help me with my problem?*

As the Hoggarth drew closer, Ryan realized it probably *was* going to eat them. Despite its pretty feathers, the Hoggarth was a monster. Part snake, part horse, part bird, and mostly dragon—it had a wingspan of twenty feet!

When the monster zoomed into a dive, Yun assumed a fighting stance, low with good balance. Ryan did the same, although his stomach was knotted with fear. The beast looked like it could tear them apart with little effort.

Yun and the Sea Serpent

Holding the blade level with his eye, Yun took aim with his sword. At the last moment, the Hoggarth veered away from them and swooped into the rocks. It perched on a craggy ledge about fifty feet over their heads.

Craning its snakelike neck, the Hoggarth looked down at them with disdain. "You are destroying my waterfalls with your ugly boat. Your punishment is death."

"I beg to differ," said Yun. "We walked around your waterfalls. We were very careful not to disturb the Zubrium."

"You saw it?" asked the Hoggarth.

The Roo bowed, keeping his hand on his sword. "I am Yun, Warrior of Virtue. Water is my element. This is my companion, Ryan."

He slapped Ryan in the stomach, and the Newcomer bowed too.

"Warrior of Virtue, you say?" asked the Hoggarth. "You might have to prove that."

"We are on the same mission," said Yun, "to restore Tao to health and glory. We were using this river to reach the Lagoon Lifespring. The river is lucky to have such a kind and powerful benefactor as yourself."

"Flattery will not help you," sneered the beast. "Prepare to die!" The Hoggarth flapped its great wings and lifted off the ledge.

"Stay close to me!" growled Yun, shoving Ryan behind him.

As the Hoggarth swooped toward them, Yun dropped his sword and squatted down. He leaped up and spun around in midair, and his giant feet caught the Hoggarth right in his stomach.

The Hoggarth squawked and flapped its wings, but it still thudded to the ground. Yun twirled in the air like a helicopter, and his robes billowed out to slow his fall. He landed on one leg, spun around and—*whap!*—his tail slapped the Hoggarth in the face.

The monster fell to its knees and howled like a banshee. Yun went spinning through the air and tried to land behind it, but the Hoggarth swept a giant wing through the air. The wing just barely struck Yun's leg, but it sent him twirling to the ground.

The monster reared up and tried to trample the Roo with its hooves. Yun just barely rolled out of the way.

"No!" shouted Ryan.

At once, the Hoggarth turned and galloped toward the boy. Ryan shrieked and dashed toward the river, hoping the water would save him. Halfway there, he tripped over a rock and plowed face-first into the dirt.

The Hoggarth landed on top of him and pinned him to the ground. A sinewy neck curled toward him, and he could see ruby-red scales on the monster's throat.

Golden eyes glared at him, and a large beak snapped in his face. "I'll eat you now, Warmblood."

Ryan kicked up with his legs and caught the monster in the stomach. It backed up a few inches, then pounced on him again. Multicolored feathers flared across the back of the Hoggarth, and it opened its beak to strike.

Suddenly a blast of water smashed into the creature and knocked it away from Ryan. With a screech, the Hoggarth flapped its wings and tried to escape from the stream. Ryan looked around, and he saw Yun, holding what looked like a fire hose.

As he looked closer, Ryan realized that the hose was really Yun's sword! It was drawing water from the stream and shooting it at the Hoggarth. The drenched beast finally got high enough to escape the water, and Yun withdrew his sword from the stream and slid it into his belt.

"The Crystalline Sword!" hissed the Hoggarth. "All right, perhaps you are a Warrior of Virtue."

With a few flaps of his great wings, the beast landed back on the craggy ledge, a safe distance away from them. It held its wings out to dry.

Yun bent down and helped Ryan to his feet. "Are you all right?"

"Yes. That was close."

"Regular weapons aren't much good against a

Hoggarth," said the Roo. "Only gifted weapons make an impression."

The winged creature chirped. "Do you know Lai?"

"Of course I know Lai, Master of Wood."

"We are from the same province," said the Hoggarth. "Is he helping you too?"

"He has his own mission," answered Yun. "He must reach the Emerald Lifespring to protect its people from the headhunters."

"Headhunters?" murmured Ryan. That sounded even worse than fighting a sea serpent."

"I will fly there and say hello to my old friend," vowed the Hoggarth. "Is there any message you wish me to pass along?"

Yun glanced at Ryan and said, "Is there anything to be done for a human who has slept in an enchanted cave? It has turned him into a Warmblood."

The Hoggarth gave a throaty chuckle. "So that is what is wrong with your companion. I sensed there was something odd about him."

"Can you help me?" asked Ryan boldly.

The monster shrugged. "To break a spell like that, you must do something unselfish. You must do something completely for others."

"Oh," said Ryan. That was probably harder than it sounded.

"And you'll have to learn a lesson," said the Hoggarth.

"I learned a lesson—never to sleep in enchanted caves!"

"That is only common sense. You must learn a *real* lesson. When the time comes, you will have my blessing." The magical being lifted his wing and pointed it at Ryan, and a streak of light engulfed him.

Ryan got dizzy and started to fall, but Yun caught him. "Thank you, mighty Hoggarth!" called the Roo.

"You are welcome." With a regal flapping of its wings, the Hoggarth lifted off into the sky. It rose gracefully over the canyon walls and was gone.

Ryan shook his head and stared at Yun. "Wow, that was strange. Do you think it's true what he said? Do you think it will really help me become human again?"

"It might," answered the Roo. "But you must supply most of the magic."

"Speaking of magic, what was that thing you did with your sword?"

"I can channel the power of water," answered Yun, "if I am standing close to it. I only did it to impress the Hoggarth."

"It impressed me too," said Ryan.

Yun rubbed his companion's head, and Ryan felt like a faithful dog. "Come on, we've rested long enough."

Moments later, they were back on the raft, floating

down the middle of the stream. Only now it was a small river, about twenty feet wide. The geology changed again, as the rock walls gave way to level land. They floated through a colorful meadow of tall, purple grain.

For the first time, they saw other people—Warm-bloods and humans, who were harvesting the grass. Ryan waved, but the people were far away, and they didn't notice the bundle of logs floating past on the river.

"What are they picking?" asked Ryan.

"It's a kind of wild rice," explained Yun. "It's good to see it growing here again."

"Shall we stop to talk to them?"

Yun looked at the sun, which was edging toward sundown. "No. We must go as far as we can today."

The last time they had stopped, the Hoggarth had shown up, so Ryan was content to float. As a Warm-blood, he was beginning to feel more connected to this wondrous land. Was that the lesson he had to learn, that Tao was cool? No, it couldn't be that simple. He already knew that.

As they floated along through the beautiful mead-ows, Ryan began to feel drowsy. Once or twice, he almost slipped off the raft. He also began to get itchy, especially the parts of his fur that hung in the water.

His ankle itched, so he kept scratching it, until his

paw felt something squishy. He tried to peel it off, but it seemed to be stuck, like a piece of chewing gum.

Ryan lifted his leg out of the water and showed it to Yun. "What is this thing on my leg?"

Yun shrugged. "These waters seem to be infested with leeches."

"Leeches!" shrieked Ryan.

"Yes. You know, bloodsucking worms."

Ryan began paddling toward the shore. "I don't want any leeches on me! I'm getting out of here!"

"Wait," said Yun, steering them back into the middle of the river with his sword. "When we stop, I'll take the leeches off. Water isn't perfect—it has its bad side too. But the water is giving us a free ride, so the least we can do is to feed some of its residents."

"Yuk!" said Ryan. "*You* feed them." He started paddling for the shore.

"That's very selfish of you," said Yun.

But the harsh words didn't change the boy's mind.

A few minutes later, Ryan sat on the bank, prying slimy leeches off his fur. He felt bad. Yun was kind to all creatures, but Ryan had to draw the line at blood-sucking worms, especially when it was *his* blood they were sucking. When he dropped the leeches on the ground, Yun picked them up to return them to the water.

Maybe I'm not cut out to be a Warrior of Virtue,

thought Ryan. *Maybe I am too selfish. I'm probably too selfish to ever get rid of this curse.* He wondered what kind of job a golden retriever Warmblood could get in Tao.

Yun looked over at him, and his scowl softened into a warm smile. "I mustn't judge you too harshly," said the Roo. "After all, you aren't from Tao, and your world is much different than ours. Since you look like a Warmblood, I forget that."

Ryan shook his head, and his ears flopped back and forth. "I'm going to let you down, I know it," he moaned. "I'm just not as virtuous as you are."

"That's not true," said Yun, kneeling beside him. "Having virtue doesn't mean that we must all be the same. Believe me, Chi doesn't like water. He would never set foot in this river, and he'd probably faint if he saw a leech. But he is still virtuous.

"All of us are brave and fearful in different ways. For example, when you met me, I was afraid to face people, because they knew I had killed someone. Sometimes we are both brave and fearful at the same time."

"Yin and Yang." Ryan yawned. "Say, you don't think we could just sneak in a little nap here?"

Yun nodded. "You rest. I'll make some repairs to the raft."

• • •

Yun and the Sea Serpent

When Ryan awoke, he was surprised to see that it was the middle of a very dark night. There was only a tiny sliver of a moon, and it hung low on the horizon like a lamp. A thread of moonlight glimmered on the black water.

Yun sat beside him, packing his satchel. "Are we ready to move?" he asked.

Ryan gaped. "Tonight? We're going to go in the *dark*?"

"Yes. The river is wide enough that I don't think we'll hit any snags. The water temperature is almost the same at night. If you are afraid—"

Ryan scowled. Those were the words he used to get Brad, Toby and the others to go on their adventures with the Warriors. He should be glad he only had to deal with leeches, not headhunters.

"Okay," said Ryan. "At least I won't be able to see the leeches."

Yun picked up the raft and showed him the railings he had made along the edges of the crude vessel. "This should keep your legs out of the water."

Ryan smiled. "Thanks."

A few moments later, they were afloat again. By night, the journey down the river was even weirder than by daylight. Ryan could hear fish and frogs plopping into the water, but he couldn't see them. A sea serpent could be right underneath, and he would never know until it was too late.

With nothing else to look at, Ryan gazed at the stars twinkling in the night sky. In the sky of Tao, there had to be a million more stars than he ever saw at home. Yet he thought he recognized some of the constellations. If they were the same stars, did that mean that Tao and Earth were really the same place?

Yin and Yang.

He looked back at Yun and saw him do a strange thing. He stuck his paw into the river.

"We need to stop," he announced. Yun turned his sword and steered them toward the bank.

As soon as they were out of the water, Yun began to fill a water bag. "The water tells me that the ocean isn't far away," he said. "We need to get fresh water now."

Ryan looked at his matted fur. "I noticed the leeches were gone. How long will it take us to reach the Lifespring?"

"Most of tonight and tomorrow."

"How are we going to get there?"

Yun gripped the hilt of his sword. "Our raft will get us there . . . with a little help."

They drifted through darkness until the first rays of golden light peeped over the horizon. Ryan stared at the dawn, and looked around. He was amazed to find that they were adrift on the ocean. He thought they were still on the river. The land of Tao was only a wisp of fog far behind them.

He had never seen an ocean that was so calm. Its dark blue surface was like glass, with just the barest ripple of a wave. There was no wind either, and Ryan couldn't figure out how they were moving. Somehow they sliced through the water as if they were in a motorboat.

He looked back at Yun and saw him guiding the craft with his sword. But he wasn't only steering—he was meditating. Behind them Ryan could see the water churning and he realized that Yun's sword was propelling them.

Ryan wanted to ask how that was possible, but he knew he shouldn't interrupt Yun. The Roo had a special relationship with water, and now the water was taking him home.

As the sun rose higher in the sky, Ryan found that he could see great distances through the clear blue water. Vast schools of tiny fish rippled beneath him, like yellow leaves on an aspen tree. Flitting between them were large creatures with bodies like basketballs and long, trailing tentacles, colored red and purple. Below the schools of fish and the odd creatures were long, dark shapes which looked like eels.

Occasionally, deep below, he saw even bigger,

darker shapes. Ryan wanted to think they were whales, but his mind was filled with sea serpents. He was afraid to ask Yun what the giant creatures were.

By the time the sun reached high overhead, Ryan was burning up with heat. Even Yun was sweating through his fur. There was no land anywhere in sight—only endless, blue ocean—and they couldn't drink any of it. Ryan sipped some water from Yun's bag, but his tongue still hung out of the side of his mouth.

For relief, he started to splash water on his fur.

"Don't do that," said Yun. "It contains too much salt. It will only dry your skin and make it worse."

"How can it be worse?" asked the Newcomer.

"We could be lost," answered Yun.

"Are we?" Ryan asked worriedly.

"No. In fact, we're almost there." The Roo reached into a tiny pouch on his vest and pulled out a wooden tube. He extended the tube, and Ryan saw that it was a telescope. Yun looked through it for a moment, then he handed it to Ryan.

"Look carefully," said Yun. "On the horizon, where I am pointing."

Eagerly, Ryan followed the Roo's outstretched paw. He stared at the horizon from one end to another, but he couldn't see anything.

"Where is it?" he asked.

Yun and the Sea Serpent

"Use your senses," said Yun. "Look at it like a Warmblood, not a human."

Ryan gazed through the spyglass again, letting his instincts guide him. This time he saw something—a slender tower rising in the distance. Even with the spyglass, he could barely see it.

It looked a long way away.

Yun grinned as he dipped his sword back into the water. "Wait until you see how beautiful it is."

"I'm ready to see anything besides water," said Ryan. He wiped the sweat off his muzzle and gazed up at the burning orb.

chapter
6

AS THEY GOT CLOSER, RYAN COULD ONLY stare at the gigantic tree of coral that surrounded the Lagoon Lifespring. With a hundred delicate fingers, the coral sculpture rose from the ocean like a plume. It looked like a splash of ice—green, yellow, blue, red—all the colors of the rainbow.

The Lifespring itself was deeper inside, and Ryan could see its phosphorescent glow, like the beacon in a lighthouse. Pools and terraces flowed from the Lifespring into a deep lagoon. In the middle of the lagoon was a fountain which shot water high into the sky, bathing the village in sparkling rain.

Yun was right. Ryan had never seen anything so beautiful.

As they got closer, he could see farther inside the Lifespring. It looked hollow, because the coral was growing all around a shimmering lagoon. The rain-drops sparkled as they fell, and Ryan realized there was Zubrium inside every drop. The entire place was bathed in rainbows.

In the branches of the coral were houses made of palm fronds. They were fanciful creations, in vivid colors, which only added to the rainbow effect. The coral grew into delicate balconies and steps.

People and Warmbloods stood on the balconies, waving. Some of them even dove into the ocean and swam toward the visitors. Although the sun was shining, there was a mist all over the Lagoon Life-spring.

Ryan could see an opening in the coral, like the mouth of a cave. As Yun guided them toward it, outrigger canoes came to meet them. Everyone in the canoes waved and shouted at them.

Soon Ryan would be meeting hundreds of new people. He only wished that he didn't look so strange. Warmbloods were normal on Tao, but it was still strange to *be* one.

The first canoe reached them, and he could see a pretty girl in the bow of the boat. Zubrium glittered in her brown hair, and she wore dark green clothes made of seaweed. She gave them a wave and a smile, and Ryan really wished he was human again. Maybe Warmbloods could also be pretty, but he doubted whether they could be as pretty as the girl in the canoe.

"Welcome!" she called. "Are more coming?"

"No," answered Yun. "Just us."

She tried not to look disappointed, but Ryan could tell she was. Heck, anybody should be thrilled to have Yun come to protect them. They must have been expecting *all* the Warriors of Virtue, not just one.

The girl threw them a rope, and Ryan caught it. He tied the rope to the soggy raft, and three Warmbloods in the canoe began to row. As they towed the raft to the lagoon, Yun put his sword away. With a sigh, he rested his head on the raft and let someone else do the work.

Another canoe drew closer, and a wizened old man with a scraggly beard leaned out. "Hey, Yun, remember me? Your old History professor?"

Yun sat up, a shocked expression on his face. "Master Witfar?"

"None other!" The old man bowed, then looked embarrassed. "I know I look older than I should, but I was captured by Komodo's men. They forced me to work in the mines—but we can talk about the past later. How are you? You look fit."

"Thank you," said Yun, "I am well. This is my companion, Ryan. He's never seen the Lagoon Lifespring before."

"We'll have to show you around," said the girl in the canoe.

Witfar grinned. "That's my niece, Hana. She can dive great distances to harvest pearls, sponges and seaweed."

"I'm only average." Her smile sparkled like the Zubrium in the water around them.

Hana, Ryan said to himself. His tail began to wag. Ryan wanted to tell her that he wasn't really a Warmblood, but he didn't think she cared. He looked like a Warmblood, and smelled like a Warmblood—so he was a Warmblood.

As the canoe towed them into the Lifespring, the soft mist from the fountain sprayed across Ryan's face. The branches of coral reached into the sky, like the fingers of a giant. People continued to shout and wave from the balconies. The entire scene was bathed in a soothing mist of rainbows.

They were in an atoll, thought Ryan, with a lagoon in the center. The coral grew all around them, encrusted with Zubrium, and the Lifespring glowed at the top of the terraces, nourishing everything.

Trees, flowers and fruits blossomed in every pool and every corner of the Lifespring. Ryan had never seen a place so full of life.

The grin on Yun's face said it all. He was beaming. "It's all growing back! It looks so wonderful!"

"Are you glad you came back?" shouted Witfar.

Yun and the Sea Serpent

Yun nodded to the old man. "Oh, yes. But now I'll be sorry to leave."

"You don't have to leave," said Witfar. "We'd be happy to take you back. We need hard workers."

Yun's face darkened. "The Warriors of Virtue must be vigilant. The forces of evil are not totally gone."

"Don't we know it," said Witfar. "That darn sea serpent—"

"Ssshhh!" cautioned Hana. "It hasn't appeared for days. Maybe it has gone away."

"Fat chance," muttered Witfar.

Soon they couldn't talk anymore, because their voices were drowned out by the shouting of the populace. Dozens of people dove into the lagoon and swam along beside them. Bells chimed high up in the towers of coral, and the rainbow mist kept falling.

Ryan and Yun were towed to a small beach, where important people stood waiting to meet them. One of the dignitaries was a Warmblood with big tusks, a mustache and a droopy face. He looked like a walrus. Suddenly, Ryan didn't feel so bad for looking like a golden retriever.

They jumped off their raft onto the beach, and the chubby Warmblood bowed to them. "Welcome to the Lagoon Lifespring. I am the mayor, Walroo, and this is my council." He motioned to the other dignitaries, and they bowed.

"We are honored," said Yun with a bow.

The mayor patted his great stomach. "Thank you for answering our call. Where is the rest of your party?"

"This is it," answered Yun.

"But the other Warriors of Virtue—"

"They're busy," said Yun. "This is not the only Lifespring with problems. Lai journeys to the Emerald Lifespring to fight headhunters. Tsun has gone to the Mushroom Lifespring, which is infested with rats. Chi has gone to the Volcano Lifespring, where there are terrible floods. And Yee braves the mountains to reach the Chrome Lifespring, which is threatened by wolves."

Headhunters, rats, floods and wolves? thought Ryan. He should consider himself lucky to be up against a sea serpent.

The people had stopped cheering, and Yun looked at them gravely. "I know you're disappointed, but the Warriors of Virtue can only do so much. To help you, I have brought with me a companion who is very wise. His name is Ryan, and he knows about things beyond this world."

Ryan gave them a little wave. "Hi!"

Hana gave him a smile, but the others just looked shocked. With hundreds of humans and Warmbloods living in the Lifespring, they were still scared to death of one sea serpent. To them, two more Warmbloods weren't enough to make a difference. They had expected an army of Rooz to come to their rescue.

"Hey!" said Ryan, trying to cheer them up. "I'm sure Yun can handle some old sea serpent. How bad can it be?"

From the looks on the faces of Walroo and the others, it must have been pretty bad.

Witfar leaped from his boat and wagged his finger at his neighbors. "Look at yourselves! Is this how we welcome visitors to our Lifespring? Don't you know that Yun was born here? He's a hero! Without him and the Warriors of Virtue, we would still be slaves to Komodo."

Walroo frowned, his droopy face looking even more droopy. "Witfar is right. I'm sorry, Yun. We don't mean to be disrespectful. Of course, we welcome you and Ryan to the Lagoon Lifespring."

"But what good will it do?" called another voice. A middle-aged woman pushed her way through the crowd. Ryan could see that her eyes were red from crying. "The sea serpent will continue to attack us. We won't be safe until we *kill* it, or give it what it wants."

"What does it want?" asked Yun.

Walroo cleared his throat. "We don't know. It promised to tell us, but it hasn't yet."

Witfar started jumping around again. "I say, forget the stupid sea serpent! At least for today. A hero has returned home, so this is a day to *celebrate*. Hail to Yun!"

"Hail to Yun!" shouted the people. "Hail to Yun!" They sounded as if they wanted to forget the sea serpent, but couldn't quite get it out of their minds.

Walroo clapped his flippers. "We will hold a parade in your honor!"

At once, people rushed to their canoes and started to form a circle of boats in the lagoon. From every branch of the Lifespring, residents waved colorful banners and flags. Grabbing flutes and drums, they began to play music. Some of them played a song, but most of them just made noise.

From this chaos, the canoes somehow began to move in the same direction. As the happy procession circled the lagoon, Hana walked over and stood beside Ryan. He looked at the girl and decided that she was probably two or three years older than him. Too bad.

Besides, thought Ryan, he should be loyal to Tracy. She might go out with him, if he ever became human again. He hoped Tracy was okay, and that she and Tsun were doing all right against the rats.

He turned to see how Yun was enjoying the parade. But the Roo wasn't even watching it. Instead he was talking to the woman who had yelled at him. He patted her on the back and seemed sympathetic to her words.

Yun and the Sea Serpent

That was just like Yun, making friends with a person who opposed him.

Ryan turned to look at Hana, and he found her gazing at him. "There's something strange about you," she said. "I can't put my finger on it. What kind of Warmblood are you?"

Sheepishly he looked down. "Can you keep a secret?"

"Sure."

"I'm not really a Warmblood. I'm a human who fell asleep in an enchanted cave."

Hana started to laugh. At Ryan's glum expression, she covered her mouth. "I'm sorry. It's not funny, is it?"

"I don't think so," muttered Ryan.

"But you're a very handsome Warmblood—for a human." She laughed again, and Ryan couldn't help but like her.

"Come on, let me show you around." Hana took his paw and led him toward some steps that had been carved in the coral.

As the canoes circled the lagoon and the people beat on their drums and bells, Hana and Ryan climbed higher into the village. They passed homes and shops, built right into the coral, with colorful palm branches. They were like tree houses, even though this wasn't a tree.

Warriors of Virtue

In the shop windows, Ryan could see paper lanterns and seawood clothing for sale. But nobody was working—they were all down in the lagoon, celebrating.

Ryan leaned over a balcony and got dizzy for a moment. Far below, shrouded in mist, the colorful banners and canoes looked like flower petals swirling in the water. It was an incredible sight.

Hana pointed to a small red house stuck between two branches of coral. "I live there with my uncle Witfar," she said. "It's not very big, but we have enough room."

"Where are your parents?" asked Ryan.

She looked down at the crowd. "They disappeared when Komodo took over. I was just a little girl, and my uncle smuggled me out. I don't remember them."

"I'm sorry," said Ryan. Everybody in Tao had stories like that, even the Warriors of Virtue. Komodo's rule had been long and brutal.

"And your parents?" she asked.

"They're far away," answered Ryan. He didn't want to tell her that he was also a Newcomer. He liked blending in, being just another citizen of Tao.

Hana pointed to a row of low buildings on the other side of the lagoon. "My school's over there. Mostly we study agriculture and marine biology. Even though plants grow well in the lagoon, we have to make sure we have enough food for everyone. More people are coming to live here all the time."

"I can't blame them," said Ryan. "It's really beautiful." He looked around at the living, growing mass of coral, bathed in a sparkling rain. *Who wouldn't want to live here?*

"I like to come up here because you can see so far," said Hana. "Let's go even higher!"

With a sigh, he followed her up several more levels. They went so high that only the finest mist from the fountain touched Ryan's fur. At the top of the Lifespring, they climbed a rope ladder and stood on a spindly branch. Ryan didn't look down. He looked up, where there was nothing but blue sky.

Ahead of him, Hana strolled along as if she was taking a walk in the park. Ryan wished he had a railing to hang on to. Luckily, he could see where they were headed—toward a blue pod of hardened coral. It looked ancient, and was cracked in half, like a broken Easter egg.

"We call this the Crow's Nest," explained Hana. She jumped over the sparkling blue wall and stood in the hollow within. With a gulp, Ryan followed her. There wasn't much room, and they had to stand close together. Ryan held on to Hana's arm, afraid he might fall out.

As he looked down from the Crow's Nest, he felt as

if he was at the end of the world. In every direction, there was nothing but blue-green sea—

Except for the black shadow moving swiftly under the water toward the lagoon.

Hana saw it too, and her body tensed. With her hand shielding her eyes, she leaned over the wall. "Do you see that?"

"The black thing? Yes, I saw those—"

She bolted past him and ran down the spindly branch. Before Ryan could even catch his breath, she was dropping hand over hand down the ladder.

"What is it?" he yelled.

"The sea serpent!" she shouted back.

He watched her run into a green building stuck between two yellow branches. A few seconds later, a loud bell began to peel. Ryan heard it clearly enough, but he was close to it. Below them, there was a party going on, and people were banging all kinds of bells and cymbals. They couldn't hear the warning!

Ryan whirled around and saw the sinewy shadow coming closer. It was about fifty feet long, and had the shape of a giant leech. In a few moments, it would pass through the opening into the Lifespring. Because it was underwater, the people in the lagoon would never see it—until it was too late.

Without thinking what he was doing, Ryan began

running across the catwalk. He leaped onto the ladder and tumbled down to the next level.

"Hey! Hey!" he shouted, but nobody paid any attention to him. They thought he was cheering, along with everyone else.

Ryan ran down a few more levels and leaned over another balcony. As he stared down, he saw the dark shape slip into the lagoon. It circled under the canoes.

Hana rushed past him, and there was panic in her voice. "We're too late to warn them!"

"Yun!" said Ryan. Maybe he couldn't make the people hear his voice, but Yun might be able to hear his thoughts.

Ryan searched for the Roo on the beach, and he finally spotted him. He closed his eyes and concentrated. *Danger!* he told Yun with his thoughts. *Danger down below!*

When Ryan opened his eyes, he saw Yun drop into a crouch. Then he saw a huge, black monster, rearing out of the water. It had scales and fins like an eel, jaws like a crocodile and whiskers like a catfish. It was the biggest, ugliest thing Ryan had ever seen.

The sea serpent lashed its tail out of the water and knocked over two canoes. Helpless people spilled into the lagoon, and the monster stared at them with bulging, red eyes. As they screamed, it opened its great mouth to eat them.

chapter 7

THE SEA SERPENT LOOMED OVER THE helpless people in the lagoon and licked its slobbering lips. Everyone seemed to be screaming and running, and Ryan was too far away to do anything. The people in the water didn't stand a chance.

Suddenly something blue flashed through the air. It was Yun. Spinning like a ball, the Roo splashed through the fountain and landed on the serpent's head. The creature reared up with its powerful neck, and sent Yun flipping. Somehow he landed on the beach and spun around.

The sea serpent lunged for Yun, and he leaped deftly out of the way. On one leg, he spun around and slapped the sea serpent six times with his tail. The creature roared and slithered away.

Yun leaped again and ran across the back of the

serpent as it tried to dive underwater. When he reached the thing's head, he grabbed its whiskers and yanked.

The beast shrieked in pain. It was such a horrible sound that Ryan had to hold his ears. The creature tried to shake Yun off, but the Roo wouldn't let go. As he gripped the serpent's whiskers, he wrapped his legs and tail around its neck.

Howling, the sea serpent dove underwater, with Yun still clinging to its back. Ryan ran down two more levels to see what was going on.

The lagoon looked as if it was boiling, as Yun and the sea serpent thrashed under the surface. Neither one of them was going to give up. Finally, the sea serpent leaped out of the water and snapped its neck like a whip. Yun couldn't hang on, and he sailed into the water with a huge splash.

Sensing victory, the sea serpent lunged at Yun, but a wave picked him up and deposited him on the beach, near his sword. Ryan blinked, hardly believing he had seen that. The water truly was Yun's friend.

The sea serpent hissed and dove under the water. It shot across the lagoon like a torpedo and plowed into the beach, but Yun jumped high into the air. He twisted around and bounced off a sharp piece of coral, landing on the other side of the monster.

With a hiss, the sea serpent whipped around and tried to grab him. Yun's sword was a blur as it slashed through the air and sliced off one of the serpent's whiskers.

The monster howled like a banshee and backed away from the Warrior of Virtue. From its wound, black blood dripped into the water. The serpent cruised into the middle of the lagoon, with water flowing off its sleek body. It wasn't going to mess with Yun again.

Ryan gulped and tried to relax. By now, the people had scrambled into the upper reaches of the Lifespring, and they were safe. Thanks to Yun's quick action, nobody had been hurt.

"Go away!" Yun shouted at the serpent. "These are good people, and they don't need you. There are plenty of fish in the sea for you to eat!"

The sea serpent hissed. "What if I don't like fish? What if I like *humans*?"

From his perch, Ryan gulped. He was suddenly glad he wasn't a human.

"I demand that you go away!" said Yun. "And never return."

"Or what?" sniffed the serpent. "I could destroy this entire Lifespring—sink it into the ocean. I can attack the farmers and fishermen whenever I want, and you can't stop me."

Yun folded his arms. "What would it take to make you go away?"

"Let me see," mused the creature. "If the villagers

furnish me with a bride—a *human* bride—I will go away. It must be the most beautiful maiden in the Lifespring." The monster lifted a fin and pointed toward Ryan. "I want *her!*"

Ryan blinked and looked around. Standing behind him was Hana. She looked very pale.

"Hana!" said someone. "All it wants is Hana."

"Yes," said another. "If we give it Hana, it will go away."

Suddenly, everyone was looking at Hana.

"No!" said Yun forcefully.

The serpent swam lazily under the fountain. "You do not live here, and you'll be gone soon. I am talking to the council and the others who live here. Tomorrow at sunset, dress my bride in a beautiful gown and set her adrift on the sea in a boat. If you do this, I will never bother your lagoon again."

"No!" shouted Ryan.

"No!" yelled Witfar and a few others. But many of the people were silent. In their terrified faces, Ryan could see how much they feared the sea serpent. The monster was right about one thing—Yun wouldn't be around forever to protect them.

"Do as I demand," said the serpent, "or I will destroy the Lifespring and eat you all!"

With a laugh, the slimy creature slid into the water and was gone. Ryan could see its dark shape ooze from the lagoon into the open sea. From a distance, it looked like a small submarine.

"Post a guard in the Crow's Nest," ordered Mayor Walroo. "We must have a Lifespring meeting."

Ryan knew the people were afraid, but he still couldn't believe they would give Hana to a hideous monster. He turned around to tell Hana that everything would be okay, but she was gone. He looked for her on the paths and branches, but she was nowhere to be seen.

An hour later, the lagoon looked like a coliseum with a fountain in the middle. Hundreds of humans and Warmbloods were gathered around, just like before. But they weren't cheering. Only adults attended this meeting, as it wasn't a matter for children.

Ryan kept looking for Hana, but he couldn't see her anywhere. He hoped she would come to defend herself against this crazy plan. There had to be some other way to deal with that rotten sea serpent, although he couldn't think of any.

Mayor Walroo and all of his council were gathered on the beach, along with Yun, Master Witfar and dozens of others. Ryan went over to stand beside Yun. The big Roo looked very stern, as if he knew his benevolence would be tested.

"They are about to do a terrible thing," said Yun.

Ryan stared at him. "They aren't really going to give Hana to that *thing!*"

"Fear makes people do strange things," said Yun. "For too many years, these people lived in fear of Komodo. Now they live in fear of the sea serpent. They would do almost anything for peace."

Walroo slapped his fins together and barked loudly like a seal. It grew so quiet in the Lifespring that Ryan could hear the tug and ripple of the water. He looked over at Master Witfar. The old man was nervously pulling on his beard.

The mayor shook his walrus tusks importantly. "This meeting of the Lifespring will come to order. We have only one matter to discuss—the sea serpent.

"As all of you know, the serpent attacked again today, spoiling the parade for our guests. The monster gave us an ultimatum. Either we send Hana to him as a bride, or he will destroy the Lifespring, and eat all of us."

Walroo looked very disturbed by such a possibility. "We must hear arguments from both sides. Hana's uncle, Witfar, has asked to speak for her. Master Witfar?"

The wizened man waved his arms. "Listen to me, please! Hana and I were born in this Lifespring, and she lost her parents here. Nobody loves this place more than Hana. You can't turn her over to the sea serpent. You simply can't do it!"

"What else are we to do?" yelled someone. Others began to shout too, and once more Walroo clapped his fins and barked like a seal.

"You will have a chance to speak," said the mayor. "Please continue, Witfar."

The old man just shook his head. "If you sacrifice that poor girl, then you are no better than the sea serpent. Plus, there is no guarantee that the monster will leave us alone. That is not an honorable sea serpent! I say we fight it, as Yun did."

More people began to shout, and Walroo had a hard time making them be quiet. "Are you done, Witfar?"

The old man nodded.

"Then I will hear from Taloon."

A Warmblood who looked like a mountain lion strode to the center of the beach. His cold eyes glanced at Yun, and his whiskers twitched.

"We all appreciate what Yun did to fight the sea serpent," said Taloon. "But he didn't really harm the beast. The serpent comes and goes as it pleases, and Yun will be gone in a few days.

"We can't protect every diver who looks for sponges, or every fisherman who goes out in his boat. The serpent can attack at any time, and we are helpless. Our only hope is to make peace with it. In our history, sea serpents have been known to keep their word.

"In short," said Taloon, "it is the life of one maiden versus the lives of all of us. I would go in her place, if I could. Hana should be willing to make the sacrifice."

"Yeah!" shouted someone. "She should do it!" Ryan felt sick to his stomach.

"May I speak?" asked Yun.

Walroo nooded, and everyone stood back to make room for the big Roo.

"Ryan and I came here to help you," said Yun, "but we didn't come here to fight your battles for you. If all of you stand together, you can defeat the sea serpent. It won't be easy, and it might take some time. But if you are virtuous, you will prevail."

"Yun!" called a woman. "Will you kill it for us?"

The Roo shook his head. "No, I will not kill it. I am convinced there are other ways to deal with the sea serpent."

"What are they?" shouted someone.

Yun shrugged. "We must think about it, and make plans."

"No!" shouted a man. "It's killed too many people already. Why do we have to wait? We can make it go away tomorrow!"

"Yes! Yes!" agreed Taloon. "We must make it go away!"

Yun and the Sea Serpent

Many people took up the chant. "Make it go away! Make it go away! Make it go away!"

Ryan looked at Witfar, and the old man's shoulders slumped. He knew that Hana's life was in grave danger. Ryan looked at Yun. If only the Warrior would agree to kill the sea serpent, the people would be happy.

But Yun would never kill again. It was against his nature. He just crossed his arms and waited.

Walroo cleared his throat. "Very well. I think that is enough discussion. The council will now vote." With his foot, he drew a line in the sand.

"Those who wish Hana to be the bride of the sea serpent, step across the line."

Ryan covered his eyes, because he didn't want to watch. But he peeked over his paw. Six members of the council crossed the line, and three didn't move. Some people in the Lifespring cheered, but not Witfar, Yun or Ryan.

"The vote has been cast," announced the mayor. "Brave Hana will be the bride of the sea serpent." He turned to Yun and said, "I'm sorry."

"Don't apologize to me," answered Yun. "Apologize to Hana and her uncle."

With slumped shoulders, Witfar started up the steps. "I will tell Hana." People stepped out of the way and let the old man pass. They looked sad, but none of them offered to go in Hana's place.

Hmmm, thought Ryan. *None of them offered to go in Hana's place.* That gave him an idea. He started across the beach to stand beside Yun.

"It's too bad I'm not human," said Ryan.

"Can't you stop thinking about your own problems?" grumbled Yun.

"I'm not thinking about my own problems. I'm thinking about Hana."

"What do you mean?"

Ryan looked around. Most of the people were returning to their homes, but he still whispered. "Hana and I are about the same size, or we would be if I was human. We both have brown hair. From a distance, if I was wearing a dress, I would look like her."

The Roo narrowed his large eyes. "Go on."

"Suppose I pretend to *be* Hana, and I go off in the boat instead of her. Here's the best part—"

Ryan smiled. "*You* are hiding in the bottom of the boat, so the sea serpent can't see you. When it shows up, you . . . you do something to it. You might have to kill it."

Yun stroked the fur under his chin. "I like this idea very much. Except for the killing part."

Ryan shook his head. "I don't know what else you're

going to do with that thing. Her uncle would have to help us too."

"There's just one problem," said Yun. "You aren't human."

Ryan frowned. "Oh, yeah. I forget that sometimes."

"But you would dress like a woman to do this?" asked Yun, sounding impressed.

"I guess I would—to save Hana."

"It's a wise plan which uses both the Yin and the Yang. By becoming female, you would use the soft side of your nature."

The boy looked at his paws. "I've learned a lot about being other things. But the way I look now, I could only pass for a girl *dog,* not a girl."

Ryan gazed up at the Lifespring sparkling at the top of the waterfall. His gaze traveled farther upward, and he thought he saw the tiny red shack where Hana lived.

"I would like to go see her," he said. "Do you think that would be all right?"

"Certainly," answered Yun. "Tell your plan to Hana and Witfar. Perhaps I could hide in the boat with her." He started to walk away.

"Where are you going?" asked Ryan.

"To find a needle and thread, the heavy kind used for sails." The Roo raced up a flight of stairs and ducked into a shop.

Ryan shook his head, confused. This wasn't the time

to be sewing, but Yun was his own Roo. He sighed and started up a different set of steps. Keeping his eye on Hana's house, Ryan climbed slowly, letting the golden mist wash over him.

Halfway up, he stopped to catch his breath. During the parade, people had been swarming over the Lifespring like ants on an anthill. Now he barely saw anyone. He could smell food cooking, so maybe they had all gone home to eat.

No, he thought. They had all gone home because they were afraid to face one another. They were ashamed over what they were doing to Hana.

These thoughts occupied his mind until he reached the little red house. The door was made from palm fronds lashed together, and he could hear muffled crying inside. Ryan rapped on the palm fronds.

There were footsteps, and Master Witfar opened the door. He stared angrily at Ryan. "What do you want? Can't you see, we are in mourning."

"I want to speak to Hana for just a moment," said Ryan. "You too."

Witfar frowned. "Why? I don't even know you. Come tomorrow—to the wedding!" He slammed the door in Ryan's face.

"What do you mean, you don't know me?" shouted Ryan. "Look, I'm trying to help you!"

"Then go away, and let us mourn in peace," came a voice from inside.

"What's the matter with them?" growled Ryan. He started to knock on the door again, but this time he looked at his hand. There was no fur on it—it was a hand, with fingers!

With excitement, Ryan felt his face and his arms, and he didn't have any fur! Well, he had that patch on top of his head, but that was okay. His clothes fit him again, and his tongue didn't hang out of his mouth.

I'm back to being human! thought Ryan with excitement. *No wonder Witfar didn't recognize me!*

What had turned him back? It must have been when he offered to go in the boat instead of Hana. An unselfish act, as the Hoggarth had predicted.

A moment later, Ryan got a knot in his stomach. If he had turned human because of his plan, then he really had to go through with it. He had no excuses. Yun would be counting on him.

Tomorrow at sundown, he would be adrift in a boat, waiting to face a horrible sea serpent. And the worst part was, he would be dressed like a girl.

chapter 8

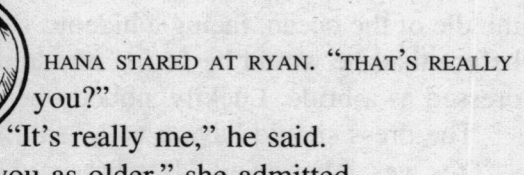

HANA STARED AT RYAN. "THAT'S REALLY you?"

"It's really me," he said.

"I pictured you as older," she admitted.

"I picture myself as older all the time," said Ryan with a shrug. "But this is what I am."

Yun swung his tail around, almost knocking Witfar off his feet. There was hardly room for all four of them to move in Hana and Witfar's little house. "This is indeed Ryan," said the Roo, "and his plan is a sound one."

Witfar stroked his scrawny beard. "Why did you wait until now to tell us? Hana is due to meet the sea serpent in only a few hours."

People were coming and going all last night and today," said Yun. "You have many friends. We had to wait to see you alone, because nobody can know about this but the four of us."

"I agree," said Hana. "But Ryan doesn't have to go in my place. I can do it, with you hiding in the canoe."

"I'm sure you could, but it was Ryan's idea. He has become human again so he could perform this unselfish act." Yun smiled. "Besides, Ryan and I are a team."

Ryan beamed proudly, then the dread sank into his stomach again. In a few hours, he would be in the middle of the ocean, facing a hideous sea serpent. And before that, he would be facing hundreds of villagers, dressed as a bride. Luckily, nobody here knew him.

"The dress should have a veil," said Ryan.

"Yes, yes, it has a veil," Hana assured him. "The best seamstress in the Lifespring gave it to me. She feels so bad."

"That is why you must live," said Yun, "because this is an unjust decision, made from fear not virtue. Can Ryan fit into the gown?"

Hana looked at Ryan and smiled. "I'm sure he can, but he won't look as good as I would."

"Fine," said Yun. "Master Witfar, what arrangements have you made for the boat?"

"I told the mayor that we should take *his* canoe. It's large and has sails. It's in the lagoon right now, and I have charge over it."

"Very good," said Yun. "Everyone thinks that my

traveling companion has disappeared, and now it's time for *me* to disappear. If I hide in the bottom of the boat, is there something you can use to cover me?"

"Yes, a reed mat."

"Very well. Hana, why don't you get the bride dressed?"

Ryan gulped, and Hana nodded. "I will."

Witfar opened the door and let a breath of fresh air flow into the stuffy pod. He and Yun hurried out, leaving Ryan alone with Hana.

She went to a footlocker near the bed, opened it and pulled out a filmy green dress, made entirely out of seaweed. Ryan figured his face was about the same color.

"This is a very brave thing you're doing," Hana said with admiration.

"I know," answered Ryan, and he wasn't talking about facing the sea serpent.

Two hours later, Ryan stood looking into a mirror on the back of Hana's door. He couldn't believe what he saw. Even without the veil, he looked like a girl! It was amazing what a difference clothing made. Ryan was the same kid he had always been, but he looked totally different in the frilly green gown.

"It's a good thing your hair is kind of long," said Hana, as she fixed his collar.

She completed Ryan's disguise by setting a peaked hat with a veil over his head. The veil completely hid his face, but he could see through the gauzy fabric. He was used to seeing brides wear white, and this dark green outfit made him look mysterious and dangerous.

"Cool!" he said. "I look like a girl superhero from a comic book."

"What is a comic book?" she asked puzzledly.

"Never mind," said Ryan. "I wonder where your uncle is."

"He wanted to stay with the canoe until the last moment," answered Hana. "He didn't want anyone snooping around. When he gets here, it's time to go."

"Yeah," said Ryan grimly. "Time to go."

Hana slipped Ryan's pants and jacket over her own clothes.

"What are you doing?" he asked.

"Putting on my own disguise," she said with a wink. "I'm going to watch this battle from the Crow's Nest."

I wish I could watch it from the Crow's Nest, thought Ryan, but he had agreed to be in the thick of it. That was only fair, because it was his idea. Ryan still didn't know what Yun was going to do with the sea serpent. How was he going to get a monster to change its ways?

The door flew open suddenly, and Ryan hid his face. Then he remembered that it was already hidden. It didn't matter anyway, because it was only Master

Witfar. The old man was also dressed in his best clothes, a shiny green suit.

He slammed the door shut and whispered, "The boat is ready, and so is our surprise guest. Ryan, you look splendid."

"Thanks," said Ryan. "I think."

"Listen," said Witfar, "you have a long way to walk to get to the boat. Just follow me. People may say hello, or they may be crying. Keep your head down, and don't talk to anyone. Walk with dignity, as Hana would."

Ryan took a deep breath, but his stomach was churning like the lagoon had when Yun fought the serpent. "Okay, let's go."

"Good luck," said Hana with a worried smile. "I would still go instead of you."

"No, this is my choice," answered Ryan. He'd sure never thought he would choose to be the bride of a sea serpent.

Witfar opened the door and led the way out. Ryan slowly followed.

The first thing he saw was the red sky and the setting sun. The dim light would help his disguise, Ryan hoped. There were people everywhere, on every balcony and branch of the coral. He tried not to look at them, even though they were all staring at him. Ryan kept his head down and followed Witfar.

On his wobbly legs, it was all he could do not to stumble. What if he fell? Hana and Witfar lived high up the Lifespring, so it was a long way down to the lagoon. Ryan was glad that he had kept his old tennis shoes on. Luckily, the dress was long enough that it hid his feet.

"It wasn't us!" wailed a woman. "We don't want you to go, Hana!"

Other people cried and wailed, and Ryan did his best to ignore them. *Dignity,* he kept telling himself. At least everyone was fooled—they all seemed to think he was Hana.

The bridal procession seemed to take hours, but finally they reached the lagoon. Witfar and Ryan walked across the sand toward a big canoe floating at the dock. Unlike most of the other canoes, this one had a mast and sails.

They walked past Walroo and the council members. Several of them said they were sorry, but Ryan said nothing.

"She won't even speak to us," moaned Taloon, sounding very sad.

"Can you blame her?" asked Witfar.

"Can we at least see her pretty face one last time?" asked Walroo.

Fat chance, thought Ryan.

Witfar quickly ushered him into the mayor's canoe.

Yun and the Sea Serpent

It was a large sailboat built like a catamaran. Ryan saw a reed mat on the bottom of the boat. There was a bulge under the mat. He was careful not to step on it as he found a seat in the bow.

"Hana is a good sailor," said Walroo. "Can she sail herself out to sea?"

Oh, no! thought Ryan. *I don't know anything about sailing! I can barely row a boat.*

Witfar scowled. "You would ask this poor, doomed girl to sail herself to her own death! How cruel are you? You must *tow* her out to sea."

"Of course," said Walroo, puffing his big chest. He pointed to two of the strongest rowers and barked, "Get a canoe and tow her out to sea."

A few minutes later, there was a canoe in front of Ryan, with a rope leading to it that the rowers tied to his boat. As the men began to row, the boat cruised slowly through the lagoon. People waved and said good-bye, but Ryan kept his head down.

As he left the Lagoon Lifespring, the boy could feel the spray from the fountain on the back of his neck. He wondered if he would ever feel it, or anything else, again. He glanced back at the Lifespring and saw people tossing flowers upon the sea.

For most of the journey, Ryan was in a daze. In the canoe ahead of him, the men rowed like demons. They wanted to get out in the ocean, leave Ryan and escape as fast as possible. He couldn't blame them.

Ryan watched the wake from his boat as it rippled across the smooth surface of the sea. He tried not to look for large, black shapes under the water, but he couldn't help it. He kept his head down and his mouth shut, even though he felt like yelling, "Take me back! Take me back!"

Finally, the rowers decided they had gone far enough. With nervous looks on their faces, they cut the rope to his canoe. Then they took off so fast that they splashed him with the spray from their oars.

Ryan looked around worriedly. He could see the Lifespring, but it looked so far away. Even though Yun was in the bottom of the boat, Ryan felt alone out there. The smooth sea was turning red, as the sun sank lower beneath the horizon.

"Yun?" he asked nervously.

"Do you see something?" whispered the Roo, who was still under the mat.

"No."

"Then keep quiet."

Ryan gulped. The veil against his sweaty face began to itch, and he wished he could take it off. But he couldn't. They had fooled the people of the Lifespring, but now they had to fool the sea serpent. Ryan wondered how old the serpent was. A hundred years? A thousand years? Maybe it was too old to be tricked.

While he was thinking about that, he didn't see a dark circle under the boat. And he didn't see it turn around and shoot toward the surface like an underwater missile.

The monster burst from the ocean with a huge splash, and reared forty feet in the air. Before Ryan had only seen it from a distance. Close up, it was even more horrible! It looked like a giant moray eel with snakelike whiskers, shark's teeth and bulging, red eyes.

"Aahhh!" screamed Ryan. He fell back in the boat, on top of the mat. Yun struggled to get up, but Ryan had him pinned underneath the mat.

The sea serpent loomed over him with thick, slobbering lips. "Hello, my pretty. That's a lovely dress. I wonder how it *tastes*!"

The monster lunged for him, and Ryan rolled out of the boat and splashed into the water. Sputtering, he grabbed the side of the canoe and held on, as the serpent rose over him.

It laughed with an evil hiss. "Oh, you want to live in *my* home—the sea. Very well, my beautiful bride."

The monster lunged for him again, but this time the mat flew up and struck it in the face. Ryan watched in awe as Yun jumped to his feet, his sword drawn.

"A trick!" snarled the monster.

As the surprised serpent tried to get away, Yun leaped high into the air. He did a flip and came down with his sword spinning. It banged against the serpent's hard scales and did little damage, as the creature lashed its tail around. It smacked Yun like a bat hitting a ball.

The Roo went sailing, and Ryan feared he would be lost. But a wave suddenly rose up and caught him gently, like a baseball glove cradling a ball. As Yun held his body like a lance, sword out in front of him, the wave hurled him back at the serpent.

The monster's eyes bulged in terror, and he dove into the sea just as Yun flew overhead. The Roo plunged his sword into the serpent's scales and flipped over. He landed in the water, which seemed to turn solid beneath his feet, and swirled his sword through the waves.

Suddenly the water in front of the serpent turned to ice, and the monster plowed into it with a loud crack. He reared up, looking woozy, and Yun jumped on top of the ice floe he'd just created. The Roo leveled his sword in front of him.

He's going to have to kill it, thought Ryan.

But then Yun's sword turned into a pulsating wall of water, and he flung it at the sea serpent. It smacked the serpent right in the head and sent it reeling toward the boat.

"No!" screamed Ryan, covering his head.

Yun and the Sea Serpent

It crashed to the bottom of the boat, and a wave washed over the canoe, nearly knocking Ryan overboard. As the boat began to sink, he scrambled away from Yun and the sea serpent. They were all going to drown out here.

Yun leaped into the boat, causing another big wave. The Roo held the serpent's jaws shut. In panic, the creature flopped around like a big fish, but Yun held tightly. Finally he raised his sword and plunged it through the creature's slobbering lips, pinning them shut.

The sea serpent tried to escape, but Yun wrestled it to the bottom of the boat. It lashed back and forth like a python, and water poured over the sides of the boat. It was all Yun could do to hang on.

"The needle and thread!" he shouted. "In my pouch!"

Ryan scrambled back into the boat and reached for Yun's pouch on his belt. He remembered that the Roo had gone in search of strong needles and thread, like they used to mend sails. He didn't know why until that moment.

As they sloshed about in the sinking canoe, with water pouring over the sides, Yun held the serpent down. Ryan finally got out a long, sharp needle and thick thread. He handed it to Yun and jumped out of the way.

The Roo smashed the serpent's head with a Tai Chi

punch which stunned the beast for a moment. While its jaws were pinned shut by the sword, Yun started to work with the needle.

Like a skilled tailor, he began to sew the serpent's mouth shut. When the monster realized what was happening, it fought like a demon. But Yun was determined, and he worked quickly. When he was finished, he pulled out his sword and let the serpent slide out of the boat.

It thrashed about in the water, trying to open its mouth. But Yun had used strong thread and double stitching. No matter what the creature did, it couldn't open its jaws. Finally it lay floating on the water, staring at Yun with hurt eyes.

"Don't look at me like that," said the Warrior of Virtue. "It's your own fault. Don't worry, you won't starve. Your mouth will open a little bit, enough to eat plankton and small fish. But you won't be eating any more people."

The Roo crossed his arms and looked stern. "If you ever bother the residents of the Lifespring again, I'll leave your mouth shut forever. If I hear good reports about you, I'll return someday and cut the stitches loose. From now on, you must live with virtue."

The miserable monster rolled over and sank deep into the ocean. Ryan had a feeling that it was going to be a virtuous sea serpent from now on.

Yun and the Sea Serpent

Yun picked up a bucket and tossed it to Ryan. "Use that to bail the water out of the boat. I'll put up the sails, and we can be home for dinner."

Ryan pushed the soggy veil off his face and grinned at his friend. "That was great! You did it, Yun!"

"No, Ryan, *we* did it."

chapter
9

"HAIL YUN AND RYAN!" SHOUTED THE people of the Lagoon Lifespring. "Hail Yun and Ryan!"

The boy stood on the beach, beaming with pride. He didn't even care that he was wearing a ruined gown made of seaweed. Beside him, Yun stood with his arms crossed. The Warrior of Virtue was the only one not surprised by what had happened to the sea serpent. He always expected virtue to triumph.

While the people were cheering the heroes, Hana came running down the steps. She dashed across the beach, grabbed Ryan and kissed him deeply. The boy turned about four shades of red.

Even Yun had to laugh. "A worthy reward."

"I watched you from the Crow's Nest," said Hana. "I never saw anybody so brave!"

Ryan looked down at the sand. "It was really Yun

who sewed the serpent's mouth shut. I was only along for the ride."

"Nonsense," said Hana. "You are both heroes. Are you sure you won't stay in our Lifespring?"

"Yes, stay!" shouted Master Witfar. Soon everyone took up the chant. "Stay in our Lifespring! Stay in our Lifespring!"

Ryan looked at Yun, and the big Roo shook his head. "Thank you, but I'm afraid we can't stay. There are problems all over Tao, and the Warriors of Virtue must be on guard."

Hana looked at Ryan. "What about you?"

"I'm sorry," he said. "I've got homework to do, and my mom is expecting me home for dinner."

"You will always be welcome in the Lagoon Life-spring," declared Mayor Walroo. "Are you sure the sea serpent won't return?"

"I'm sure," said Yun. "A few years of eating nothing but plankton will teach it virtue."

"We will have a feast in your honor!" bellowed Walroo. "Bring out the food!"

They ate well that night, and slept even better. In the morning, Walroo gave them his big sailboat—all repaired—and they set sail for the mainland.

As they glided over the glistening water, Ryan wondered about his friends, Tracy, Chucky, Toby and

Yun and the Sea Serpent

Brad. They had to face headhunters, rats, floods and wolves in a strange land, and he hoped they would be all right. Of course, they had the Warriors of Virtue to help them.

He looked at Yun, and the Roo was frowning. He adjusted the sails to try to capture more wind and increase their speed.

"What's the matter?" asked Ryan.

Yun lifted the blue medallion he wore around his neck. It was glowing. "I fear for Lai and Toby," he said. "At this moment, they face the headhunters, and they are a terrible foe. Even Komodo had to bargain with them."

Yun looked grimly at his medallion. "Lai, Tsun, Chi or Yee—one of them needs our help. But we won't know which one until we get back."

"I see," said Ryan, suddenly worried. "But my friends will be okay, won't they? They're with the Warriors of Virtue."

Yun smiled. "Yes, virtue goes with them."